It Is Knud Who Is Dead

Robert Zola Christensen

Translated from the Danish by
Nina Sokol

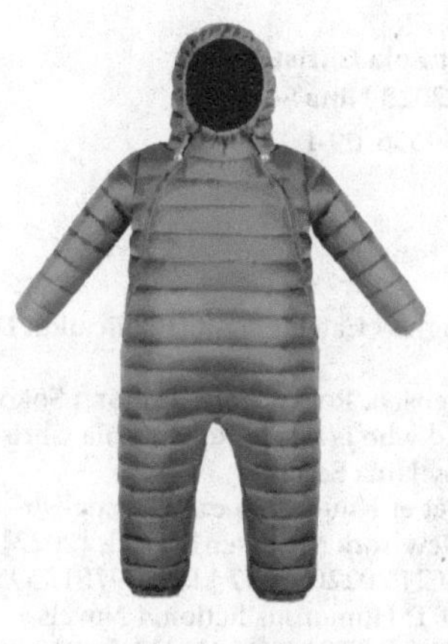

SPUYTEN DUYVIL
NEW YORK   PARIS

Library of Congress Cataloging-in-Publication Data

Names: Christensen, Robert Zola, author. | Sokol, Nina, translator.
Title: It is Knud who is dead / Robert Zola Christensen ; translated from
  the Danish by Nina Sokol.
Other titles: Det er Knud, som er død. English
Description: New York : Spuyten Duyvil, [2023]
Identifiers: LCCN 2022053647 | ISBN 9781959556091 (paperback)
Subjects: LCGFT: Humorous fiction. | Novels.
Classification: LCC PT8176.13.H7355 D4813 2023 | DDC
  839.813/74--dc23/eng/20221104
LC record available at https://lccn.loc.gov/2022053647

The Poop Doesn't Fall Far from the Dog

My Mother Is Soon Going to Die,

which is perhaps not a bad thing because we are now going to take all her savings, at least the portion that she had hidden in the safe deposit box in the bank, Handelsbanken, which is located on the pedestrian street. In a way, she gave them to us herself because she started drinking again and that was after she had been on the wagon for over three months which was a new record for her. It is her guilty conscience that has compelled her to suggest that we take care of her money now, I assume.

You'll be getting them anyway, she has said several times, and I have taken the train all the way from Amager so that we could hold this "family meeting" of ours.

I could really use the money.

We are drinking coffee and there are small Christmas decorations everywhere in the low-ceilinged living room.

So, you'll be spending Christmas at the folk high school? my sister asks even though she knows the answer perfectly well.

Yes, I will.

She nods sympathetically.

My sister is small and chubby and has a concerned

look on her face. She always does. I really like my sister. She is a good person.

She lives in the tenement block just across the street. It has these terrazzo echoing hallways which you'd think don't exist anymore, but they do here. The buildings back then were built for the workers at the steel works. It's just next door.

It's important that I come because there is also the issue with Sita. You have to feel sorry for the dog. It's lying on the floor looking up at us as though it understands that we're talking about it. Every now and then it will jump into my mother's lap, sniff at her breath and jump back down on the floor. I think I know what that's all about. The poor animal has to constantly assure itself that there's no alcohol on her breath because if there is then all hell will break loose. It's learned that the hard way because when my mother drinks she loses contact with everything around her. Then she just sits around gulping red wine from big wine glasses. And then things tend to take off from there. Sita will start wandering around whimpering in the dark apartment on the ground floor. She's neither let out in the little garden or given her routine pee-walk.

But that's not all. There's more. One of the neighbors who has every so often looked after the dog when my mother's had one of her blackouts claimed my mother must have bitten Sita. That sounds like a bad joke: "Man bites Dog." But it's true that the mark it has on its back could resemble something caused by human teeth. My mother has told us it must have happened in connection with an electric trimmer when Sita was at the groomer's not too long ago. But if you look more closely you'll notice that there's no real penetration in the lower part of the wound and my mother, well, she's actually missing most of her teeth in her lower jaw.

That's also why we've come, my sister and I. We want to take the dog away from her. Enough is enough.

I don't know what to believe but you probably have to have experienced alcoholism in your life to understand that it could manifest itself with some pretty wild results. I can just envision it. She probably went out like a light, but was still able to open her eyes and happened to catch sight of the dog lying there, snug asleep next to her in the bed. Whereupon the devil got into her: Damn it, I'm going to bite it, she thought. Why not? And then she did it, using her jaws until she pierced the little animal.

It may be that the dog is able to control its bladder so as not to urinate on the carpets but my mother, on the other hand, certainly isn't. She has managed to urinate so much in her bed that the stench is noticeable immediately upon approaching her bedroom. At other times she has been known to shit in her couch whereupon she digs the excrement out from somewhere between her legs and smears it across the wall paper where the little Christmas ornaments now are hanging.

The neighbor once contacted my sister because my mother was staggering around completely plastered in the common area with her naked big, pear-shaped pensioner's ass for all to see. According to my sister, she was trying to get into contact with the men who passed by and when they didn't respond she would get enraged and then she'd attempt to lure them by interchangeably saying sweet things to them and bawling them out.

After that episode they don't' want to see her in the Senior Citizens' Club again.

*

Come on, Sita, sweetie! My mother says as she opens the door to the garden.

The little dog pricks up its ears, scampers around on its tiny paws as it wags its tail. Stops and jumps up and down a little as though it is somewhat surprised by the cold snow covering the grass, yes, come on, girl! Good girl, yes, that's it!

My mother is really making an effort to show how good the dog is doing in her care because she'll of course do anything to keep the dog. She's asked about my new job in order to talk about something else. So you're starting on Monday? Where will you stay? At the Folk High School? And that's in Jutland, you say? Yes, Mom, the Folk High School is in Jutland and Jutland is also a place in Denmark.

I get so easily annoyed with her, but she is, when it comes down to it, just lonely, and I do, of course, somehow feel sorry for her and, Mom,: I love you, as only a child can love its mother, all those sandwiches with banana slices you've made for me. But that's many years ago. You are no longer yourself because the alcohol has taken command of you. That's how it goes, sooner or later.

I once saw a program about some ants that got some terrible parasites inside of them. The ants acted pretty normally in the beginning but it wasn't long before the small parasites took over their brains and made them behave like zombies and eventually they got their hosts to crawl up onto a blade of grass so they could be eaten by a bird or a grazing animal, a goat, for example, so that the parasites in that way could continue their cycle.

And let me tell you that the alcohol is really leading you around in circles, Mother, It was only last Christmas that I was driving through the vast darkness of Zealand with the car full of Christmas presents, my two sons and a small Christmas tree because we were going to celebrate Christmas with you, mother, Dad had died the previous summer and you shouldn't sit alone for Christmas, and I myself was in the middle of a difficult divorce. When we got to your place you had collapsed on the couch salivating with your mouth halfway open and a tiny charred roast pork was on the kitchen counter because the alcoholism you were suffering from made you not only to search for but to find and drink all the residuals, all the leftover drops you had convinced yourself you had poured out in the sink. But you were full of it because you knew quite well that you could put it away when put away time came round again.

And you opened your eyes as we stood there in your living room peering at you, at first there was a moment of confusion and perplexity on your part, what in the world have I done? And then you transformed immediately afterward into this defiant and evil creature full of hate which you only see in alcoholics who are crawling their way up to the top of the blade of grass.

*

The dog wants to go back inside now even though he's practically just been let out. It's probably extremely cold for the little creature. And it might very well not be impossible, but what do I know, that she might have been forgotten out there. That she might have had to wait by the garden door without being let in.

During my entire adult life, my mother has had a tendency to get the same very cheerful but somewhat confused Scottish terriers and since she's always tended to talk to them in the same way it's perhaps not so strange that they have gradually become replicas one of one another.

My mother gets up and lets Sita in, whereupon she goes out to the kitchen and starts opening and closing drawers, she seems to be rummaging around for something. When I hear the lid being removed from the coffee can I know that she's going to put up some more of the sour tasting coffee from Aldi, I drink the last drops that are left in my cup. It tastes like hell, to put it in plain Danish, practically like a German supermarket. But it's good considering that price, as my father used to say, I've never met anyone who drank as much coffee as my parents and they always bought the one on sale that you could find on the pallets in a discount store.

Many years ago I tried to make it clear to them, I even wrote down the calculations on a piece of paper for them, how little they actually saved by buying that particular brand. It was a summer afternoon when my father was still alive and we were sitting out in the sun up in Sjaellands Odde and were drinking that very same sour German coffee. Back then they were happy and Raffi was running around out in the yard barking at the customers who were selecting vegetables from the old platform truck which my parents had painted and placed in front of the the old fisherman's cottage which they had bought and used as a summer house. They were selling vegetables, "organic vegetables" as they wrote on their homemade placards. Part of what they sold originated from the vegetable section of Aldi where they also bought their coffee. They took the carrots and leeks home with them, unpacked them, rubbed a little soil on them and repacked them. It worked beautifully with absolutely no problems arising there because of course the Copenhageners didn't detect a single thing. Those were good times, wonderful times, I've never seen my father so happy as when he emptied the 10 and 20 kroner coins lying in the little money chest.

I remember calculating the coffee prices as they cheated like there was no tomorrow. Look here! I said. If you were to buy that Cafe Noir brand which you like so much your coffee budget wouldn't even increase by 75 DKK a month which amounts to a couple of bundles of carrots and two trays of strawberries. And I could tell that they were thinking it over. No more sour coffee, I thought, because I was certain that it had sunk in. But I was sadly mistaken because the next time I visited pot after pot of the sour German coffee was served.

*

Now it'll soon be Christmas again and, if you think about it, this whole thing about ruining Christmas and other holidays is a classic among alcoholics, it's really just a matter of staying away then. But you can't always do that. Like when, for example, my father lay dying at the hotel for patients at the Rigs hospital because of the brain tumor he had. They had apparently managed to sever some nerves or damage the nerve fiber mistakenly when they attempted to cut out the tumor because he basically lost the ability to use his limbs. Once a day we would transport him through the underground basement system to get radiation treatment at the Oncological Department over at the Rigs hospital.

After the operation all he could so was lie there and stare up at the ceiling in his hospital bed, it wasn't exactly a pretty sight, his mouth was crooked and there were black stitches on the top of his shaved head, and now we're getting at the heart of it because on one of the last afternoons of his life he complained of the fact that his Little Sweet Sanne, as he always used to call my mother, constantly had to go down for a smoke. I said to him in a nice way that she had every right to do so. Considering that she was caring for her sick husband round-the-clock, it didn't seem so unreasonable.

"But she does it a-a-a-lll the time," he stuttered.

"Maybe she does, but there's nothing wrong with it," I insisted.

But I had much to learn. Aunt Tulle was the one who suddenly revealed to me what had actually been going on at the hotel for patients. She pulled me aside at my father's funeral a few months later.

But you already knew it without wanting to face it, or what? Don't try convincing yourself that you thought she was dry and in a good period because of course she wasn't. When she went down for a cigarette it wasn't only to smoke but also to drink. She probably went back up to him completely plastered like a bear with a sore head and sat dangling from a blade of grass as he lay there like someone starting to turn into a vegetable in his bed and staring up at her as she walked in circles in the somewhat too large hotel room showering him with curses. It's unbearable to think about because when we weren't there he was left to her devices, just like Sita is now in the dark apartment on the ground floor.

Then again. I must have known, had my suspicions, because when I took the elevator down and pushed the heavy metal bed through the gray basement where the colored stripes on the asphalt floor, green, yellow, blue and red, indicated the direction, yes, well, I did notice the empty brown bottles then which "someone" must have left there.

But anyway, he died, which was why my mother sold the fisherman's cottage and bought an apartment in the town of Frederiksværk from whence they came and the nice big sum of money that was left over she placed in a bank box down on the pedestrian street. So that she could really start gaming the system and milking it dry. Among other things on her wish list were new teeth, something she hasn't gotten yet, a little extra help with the heating bills, and a pair of reading glasses. She is really slurping it in but I can't get offended by that, I really can't, especially when you think of how those on the other end of society are just grabbing everything for themselves, but the poop seldom falls far from the dog, as they say.

Should we be going? I ask my sister because we'd better just get down to the pedestrian street. That money won't exactly find its way into our pockets on its own, after all.

Yes, okay, she says.

We've pretty much gotten what we need, I say as I hold up my hand in which I am holding the shiny key to the bank box and the small slip where I have written the code: 2295.

We don't have to speak with the bank personnel at all when we get down to the bank but I know perfectly well that it'll be like going through Customs. It doesn't make a bit of difference whether you are carrying too much or not because you're always going to look like someone who doesn't have a clear conscience. And you always feel slightly guilty, anyway.

My sister goes out in the little dark hallway and

starts putting on her low cowboy boots. She groans. She's gained weight again, I go out to her in the hallway but then she stops what she's doing and goes to the bathroom.

Well, we're off then, I say to my mother who has remained sitting on the couch. She's lit a cigarette. She had otherwise stopped smoking inside.

Finally my sister comes out from the guest bathroom and starts all over again working on the tight boots. The dog pricks up its ears and barks a few times when I open the main door and some fresh air blows in.

No, you're not coming with us, I say. You'll stay here and keep an eye on mom.

My sister pushes me a little forward so she can get to her big gray jacket.

I wave at my mother before going out through the door.

She waves back but looks rather sulky, I have to admit.

I'm holding my backpack tightly, of course I am. My knuckles are practically completely white.

I walk alongside the boring backside of the NordCenter Mall where the trucks back in with goods for the stores and I continue down toward the station.

My sister has already driven off, we had only just

left the bank when she had to get going. Things couldn't happen fast enough for her.

I had asked her if she could drop me off at Hillerød on her way to Copenhagen where she was going to meet with her girlfriends. Then I could take the train from there.

Unfortunately, that hadn't been a possibility because she was already late. It's Friday, you know, she had said.

On Fridays it's the usual Pisang Ambon and tapas with her divorced girlfriends. They are four or five women who support one another morally and try to party it up a little in the weekends.

It had been really strange sitting there in the bank basement in the little cubicle dividing the many thousand-crown bills that smelled like money in the way only money can smell. It was almost solemn. One for me, one for you, one for me, one for you. There was actually quite a bit for each of us, my sister and I, and, like I said, the money landed in a dry spot as far as I'm concerned.

Still, I didn't really like it. I think my sister sensed that because she repeated several times that I myself had also heard Mother say that she had given them to us.

There were also some pieces of jewelry in the bank

box but we left them there. They weren't what we had come for. That hadn't been part of the agreement. I also noticed some securities and other documents. Most of them had been adorned with my father's snazzy signature which went well under the line in both ends. When I was a boy, he would sit at his writing desk and ever so carefully practice that damn signature. That big twerp actually believed that sort of thing made a difference. That's why my name is Allen-Bertram. An impressive name, a big name with a hyphen, the whole works. I don't really know. I've always felt that that name is a bit too big, like a big, ugly winter jacket that I've been forced to waddle about in.

*

When I turn at the obtuse corner by the center kiosk and the powder works I take a quick glance among the trees, I know what I'm searching for: the old open-air swimming pool by the City school which had been covered with a big, white larva-like plastic bubble so that it also could be used in the winter time. But it's no longer there. It was in the "bubble" as we used to call it, that I learned to swim when I was attending primary school. I smelled of chlorine for days afterwards following each swimming lesson because the kids used to urinate so much in the pool that extra chlorine had to be poured into it. The bath attendant's name was Peter and we used to call him pool-Peter, of course.

It was also here where I used to buy ice cream during the summer when I got a little older and the cover was removed. It was after they had built the new swimming pool at the Frederiksværk stadium. I started exploring the different flavors of ice cream that they had then: Kung-Fu, Copenhagen Cone, Quick Quench, Rascal and Treasure Chest.

It's strange because it seems to me that most people say that everything seems smaller than they remember when they return as adults to their hometown. But that's not how I experience it at all.

It is, of course, a while since I've been here, but it's as though everything seems more imposing, as though the past is clinging to the things I see today, making things seem bigger. It's eighteen years ago since I lived here in my hometown and a lot of good and bad things have happened to me, which goes for anyone who has grown up somewhere.

I'm not romanticizing that which once was, as many people do. My father, for example. He was known to get a little nostalgic. We were once on a special charter trip in southern Italy and during the entire trip he walked around sniffing and talking about a wonderful aroma from the old days which was everywhere. The day before we left we realized it was because they were still driving in cars that ran on lead-gasoline and that was the smell that reminded him of days gone by and, boy, did we laugh at him.

But I see the lumber yard now, which means I'll soon be at the station.

Another Train Just Left

but what does it matter when you're in good company? And, anyway, I'm not in that big a rush. Lone won't be showing up at the door to my new apartment until 8 pm sharp together with our joint offspring, whereupon it'll be time for me to play the role of weekend daddy.

And now that I through sheer randomness happen to have run into Amina at Hillerød station it would be a little strange if we didn't have a drink or two together even though she has ordered non-alcoholic gløgg. We were, after all, sweethearts all through the second year of high school. And perhaps also a little bit of the third year, all depending on how you look at it.

She is going to take the small local train, known as "The Pig" up to Hundested where she apparently still lives together with Tom who was a year ahead of us in school. I clearly remember him.

You two have been together for quite awhile now, haven't you?

She nods,

Well, congratulations, then.

Thanks.

It strikes me that that is how things always turn out in the provinces: long church weddings which are followed by childbirths and birthdays in which the obligatory soup—roast—ice cream menu is served. Most couples in the big cities get separated eventually. Like me and Lone, for example.

Then I ask her how things are going with her parents and she tells me that they still live in in the house in Østerbjerg, the little whistle stop before Hundested and according to her own account they are doing well even though her father's hearing has really deteriorated.

Well, it happens, I say, meanwhile thinking to myself that it was already bad back then. He was as deaf as a doorpost.

She asks how things are with my mother and I answer, a little too abruptly, that things are going well, even though they could be better. I don't feel like delving into her alcoholism. That topic's no fun. On the other hand, Amina and I have really managed to cover most of our shared history together and I'm beginning to understand more and more why we became sweethearts back then. Our conversation flows effortlessly. We've even had the wherewithal to laugh over the thing with Tom even though she was the one who probably laughed the most.

Back in the day, Tom was an annoying curly-haired guy who would, every now and then, come sniffing around and make advances to her. Although he didn't seem all too threatening at first, he finally managed to ruin everything. I don't feel like going into all the details because the point that I want to make really has to do with something entirely different. And that is that we are able to talk about all of these things completely openly because we don't hold any grudges, we're not clinging to some notion of sharing a future together like we did back then. We are adults now and it's no longer of any importance whether or not the curly-head went over to her place on that particular night as I had feared he had. That is, before we had actually broken up.

Okay, so it seems he did, and maybe that wasn't so great, but let bygones be bygones because I'm actually really starting to like this light, straightforward sense of honesty.

Yes, we need more of that, so I mention in passing that she had actually never really been my type.

You actually weren't the kind of girl I ever thought I'd be interested in, I say.

Amina smiles and says that she had actually been well aware of that all along.

I mostly go for girlish girls, I confide to her. I don't mention the fact that she back then as well as now would be considered slightly Balkan-chubby. She is from the former Yugoslavia even though the story back then was that she came from Italy. It was something her father had come up with. He had come up here when times were good, yes, well, if you think about it, he actually contributed to the welfare my parents' generation had enjoyed, but that's a different story, because her somewhat heavy breasts bulging out under her knitted sweater aren't my cup of tea either.

Even though they they actually look a little bigger than I remember them, they are still banana-shaped, which I don't go for.

I point at my empty bottle and jump down from the tall chair.

She smiles and nods. I walk among the winter-clad train passengers up to the counter to buy another snow-beer. I have, of course, taken my back pack with me, I won't let it out of my sight.

As I'm waiting for it to be my turn I look out at the snow cascading onto the platform and the long trains that come and go. I ought soon to get on one of them. It won't do coming too late because otherwise Lone's irritation, which is always simmering just below the surface, will erupt full scale. It's almost gotten to the point where I suspect her of just waiting for me to make one wrong move so she can let off her steam.

Amina is preoccupied with something on her telephone. She does look pretty good. True, she's gotten a little more round even though it's hard to see underneath the big blue sweater she's wearing with the turtle neck. She may very well have knitted it herself. That's what she did in our high school years, at any rate, knitted, and I remember that she knitted a pair of hippie-like socks for me which were perhaps a little outdated at that point.

We were very susceptible back then, so in that way the '70's continued to live on in a small pocket in Frederiksværk way into the 90's, which is kind of a fun thing to think about. But there was a good explanation for this. We belonged to the first classes of the newly built high school in Frederiksværk, and most of the teachers employed there were still young, and for some reason an aura of flower-power was still attached to them which in turn influenced us.

Okay, Amina feels that she's being observed. At any rate, she's looking up from the telephone with her full, cheerful looking face. She's actually glowing like a goddamn Christmas tree. I spontaneously point up toward the menu hanging behind the two busy girls wearing elf-hats serving in the hot-dog stand just to see whether she's sure that she doesn't want anything else. But she does, actually. She nods. With a big smile.

Well, that's great.

Now it's my turn, and I fish out a one thousand crown bill from the thick envelope in the inner pocket of the back pack and hand it over the counter: here you are! The first one has now been broken. The girl looks at the beautifully crinkled bill with surprise.

Guess you don't see one of these everyday? I say.

And there are actually 175 more of them I feel like adding, which of course, I don't—

Those Two Christmas Beers Were Just What Amina Needed,

I must say, because now we've started exchanging little sweet stories of the kind that you normally don't share with the opposite sex. But we can, Amina and me, because we're in that very special situation of having once been intimate while having the proper distance today. I believe, without really being able to explain it, that that is what has created this very special chemistry between us.

I have, for example, told her about the time I had just gotten married to Lone, she was actually pregnant with Rasmus, and we had gone to the summerhouse with Asger and his then girlfriend to celebrate New Year's Eve. We had ended up having sex next to each other on the living room floor after it had struck midnight. On a synthetic carpet that gave me some horrible burns which are still visible as tiny, almost indiscernible bruises on my knees. After the breakfast the next day we drove straight home and that weekend has never been mentioned since.

What about you? You must have done some wild things? I ask because I don't think that Amina has really contributed with anything interesting.

She smiles. Touches her hair.

Well, I may have, but I'm not exactly proud of it all. There are some things that are best left unsaid.

But those might be the very things that are the most interesting?

It's as though she takes a run-up. Then she tells about the time she turned 17 and her father's sister and her husband who had come from Jutland had given her some rather transparent underwear as a birthday present.

"Yeah, well, who's ever heard of such a thing? I mean, giving their niece underwear as a birthday present," I say, even though it doesn't sound all that exciting.

But fortunately there is more, because Amina tells about how when the other guests left her uncle had gone down into her room where she was getting ready to go to bed. In actuality, he and her aunt were staying in a trailer they had parked just outside the street, he wanted to see how it looked on her. The underwear.

"Wow. I actually think I can remember him. Wasn't his name Milovan?"

"Yes."

She recounts how Milovan had gone over to her gift table, the dresser in her room, and picked up the panties. As he held them between his thumb and index finger he said something along the lines of that they hadn't exactly been inexpensive and so it would be kind of nice to know whether or not they fit. So if she'd just jump into them, that would be great. And if she didn't fit them then there wouldn't be anything to do about it, but at least he'd know that he'd have to take them back and exchange them for something else.

Expensive? As far as I recall he was working at Bilka, in the produce section, and everything they brought was always from Bilka. He had probably just snatched them from one of the storage rooms because that's how he was. Fucking stingy. I suddenly recall Amina's father getting slightly annoyed because they had just barely parked their car on the street when Milovan came running with a very long wire and a plug in order to find a socket from which he could milk electricity from the house.

What about your parents? Did they ever suspect anything?

She shakes her head.

No, her father, who was as deaf as a door nail, probably didn't hear a thing.

It's not so uncommon for girls to have experiences like that.

I can imagine, I answer.

I'm just about to ask whether she ended up having to

do it when she asks me whether I remember the Waffle Corner.

Yes, I clearly remember it, I say, and I actually do. It was located in a Skagen-yellow house near the ferry going toward Rørvig and right by the pathway leading down to the beach. It must be a gold mine, my father, who was always preoccupied with that sort of thing, used to say. They would bake their own crispy waffles and they weren't stingy with the whipped cream or the extra goodies on top. And the ice cream scoops themselves were way bigger than those small ones you usually get in the big cities.

So, what about the Waffle Corner?

I understand that she is about to divulge more confidential information, which she does.

She tells me how she worked there during the summer right before she was going to start high school, and the guy who owned the shop liked to stop by and see how things were going. Every Friday, as she was finishing up, cleaning and wiping off the machines in the shop, he would leave a 100 kroner bill next to the cash register as an extra bonus.

That sounds pretty good.

Yes, except one Friday the owner hadn't left a 100

kroner bill but a 500 kroner bill instead and had then left the shop without saying anything.

I see.

So, dumb as I was, I took the bill because I assumed it was meant for me.

Of course you did.

So the following day I bought a green summer jacket which I had had my eyes on for a long time but which was, in fact, much too expensive.

Pause.

And that was something I should never have done.

Why not?

The following Friday the owner appeared after closing hours and started screaming and shouting about how his money had suddenly disappeared. I had to come clear. I had to tell him that I thought that the money had been intended for me.

I see.

But it hadn't been and no matter how one looked at it in his view I had stolen the money. And before I could defend myself he already began threatening to call the police and that he'd of course also have to call my parents.

My god! I can see where all this is going, it's a trap, and when I think of Amina's father, one thing is he might have been deaf but he most certainly wouldn't have been enthusiastic if it came out that his Serbian princess was stealing money from the cash register at her work. Amina must have felt very pressured.

What a pig, I say. So what did you do?

The owner insisted that it would be very difficult for him to just let the incident pass because that simply wasn't in his nature.

So I cried, of course, promising him that I would be sure to pay him the entire amount back, I just didn't have the money right now. I begged and pleaded but he would have none of it.

We both take a sip of our beers. She has a thoughtful expression in her eyes, as though she isn't quite certain whether she wants to tell the rest of the story. But in for a penny, in for a pound.

So what happened? What did he do then?

I don't know exactly how, but suddenly he said, in so many words, that if I pulled down my jeans, including my underwear, and leaned across the counter maybe we could find a solution together in the way of a little spanking.

Amina looks very shameful.

I see, I say.

We sit for a moment.

So you went along with it, in other words? I ask.

She slowly nods, looking down at her hands.

I suddenly realized how disgusting he really was but also saw an opportunity to just get it over with she says as she gets up to leave.

I'll have to go to the ladies' room now, will you keep an eye on my bags while I'm gone?

Of course, I say. No problem there. None whatsoever.

And then she disappears behind the bathroom door that can only be unlocked with a key that you borrow from the sausage stand. A big wooden block is tied to it so you don't forget to deliver it back.

It's stopped snowing and I could actually use another beer.

Why does everything have to be such a drag?

It Sure Is Taking A long Time!

I hope she returns from the bathroom soon because I'd really like to hear the rest of that story. Why, I myself was at that very same birthday party where she got that laced bra and matching underwear as a present, and it's true, the whole thing was far too see-through. We were seeing each other at that point, it must be, what? Over twenty years ago? Yes, in fact, it was. I sense a strange sort of warmth start to spread through the pit of my stomach, a kind of fascination, which shouldn't be there, but there you go, because what did Amina actually take part in back then?

As far as I remember, not much happened. We watched some television, Amina and me, in the living room after most of the guests had gone home. She seemed happy and content, I'm fairly sure. There wasn't any sign to indicate anything else. It had been a nice day, hadn't it? The family members had come from all four corners of the world for this birthday party as is so often the custom in Yugoslavia and Italy. A couple of neighbors had been there, too, as far as I recall. It was a real bash of a party, not just your usual birthday cake and songs.

Her mother, whose name I can't remember, but

which doesn't really matter, was out in the kitchen doing the dishes together with Amina's aunt.

And who do we have left? Her father and Milovan sat outside on the patio drinking Slivovits because no matter how much they tried to give the impression of being Italian, they always ended up drinking plum schnapps during festive occasions.

Finally, here she is.

I smile to her and she sits down and says something or other about Christmas, as though the subject we were talking about a few moments ago just suddenly vanished and her thoughts are now focused on something entirely different. She has, of course, regretted telling me all those things but that's just too bad because I have some questions now that I'd like to hear the answers to.

You did it, didn't you?

She looks at me somewhat perplexedly.

Is she being flirtatious now? Is that what she's doing?

You tried on the underwear and the bra just as Milovan told you to. And you let him look at you, didn't you?

She smiles. Then she says it wasn't exactly one of her proudest moments, I have to understand that. But things aren't always so simple and sometimes you get sucked into something that just sort of grows and grows and eventually gets out of control. And that turned out to be just the beginning.

Okay, I say, wanting to say a whole lot more, yet I don't really feel like I should act offended. That would be wrong. I'm not really sure how to tackle this, then again, I really do have a right to know. Everything. She probably cheated on me. And she is in a way actually implying that there is more to the story than what she's told me so far. I sense that she needs to get what happened off her chest.

At that very moment I look up at the clock hanging on the wall which tells me it is now 45 minutes to the hour of ex-wife.

Damn. I get up and say that I have to run, which I do, run through the door. I hear her call my name, but there's just nothing to do about it. I simply have to leave this very moment even though my bladder needs to be emptied right about now.

I Just Manage to Hurl Myself into the Train

before it starts moving. I lean back in the plastic seat and shut my eyes. With a little bit of luck and if the train stays on schedule I should be able to make it just in time. It'll all be okay. I feel bad about having to leave so suddenly like that, but what else could I have done?

I hear a couple, well up in years, sitting some seats away from me who are discussing where they should go for their winter vacation. Where she would prefer sunshine and beaches because it would be good for psoriasis which apparently has a tendency to flourish on her lower leg, he would prefer a big city and some culture.

I look out the window. It truly does grow dark early this time of year. The apartment complexes we pass have Christmas stars hanging in the windows and twinkling trinkets on the balconies.

At Allerød Station a tall man wearing an Icelandic sweater the shoulders of which are sprinkled with snow gets on board. He sits down close to where I'm sitting and smells of cold smoke.

I close my eyes and sense the train rocking as it makes its way toward Copenhagen. I am tired and half-drunk but my mind is working at full speed. I see Amina before me, she leans over the pensioner's knees and gets a couple of hard smacks on her behind and it probably wasn't beneath him to take the opportunity to examine her between her legs, either. She just had to accept that as part of the deal. She should just never have taken the man's money. She got what she had coming to her.

But what about the birthday party? I was there. We sat in the living room watching TV when Milovan showed up by the garden door, I remember now, looking at Balkan-chubby Amina with an open and utterly uninhibited expression in his eyes. He had a cigarette in his hand. Yes, that's right, back then people still smoked indoors. It's hard to imagine now, but they did. At any rate, I myself was on my way home because there were certain things that you absolutely didn't do, back then. Sleeping over at your girlfriend's place was totally out of the question so I didn't really get a chance to witness what happened there afterward. I envision myself standing in the scullery next to a humming oil heater in my childish blue rubber boots. Amina quickly kisses me on the mouth. See you, she says. She kisses me on the mouth and goes back into the house to get ready to go to bed when Milovan knocks on the door and asks her to try on the underwear. Did he go out when she changed to put them on? Probably not. Did he straighten it out and touch the material and her bare skin? Most likely. What couldn't have transpired as I sat in complete ignorance on the local train, "the pig," on my way back to Frederiksværk with her kiss still burning on my lips?

And what happened afterward? All the things she seemed prepared to tell me.

I take out my telephone, open the Facebook app, we're friends, me and Amina, so I click on her profile because I'd like to know more about her.

The first thing I see is that the entire family is busy painting a playhouse out in their backyard. One of the girls, the oldest, has an exceptionally elongated head. She's probably the one Amina is having trouble with, I thought she said something about that at one point.

It's is evident that they are in Ringsted, with grandma and grandpa.

Tom has grown dull-looking and bald. What happened to all the curls, Tom? From what I gather, he's become a shop foreman at Kærby machine station which his father founded back in the day. He maintains tractors and combines harvesters and that sort of thing. He was a very practical and bear-like guy who hardly said anything but who, when he got angry, would get seriously angry. Perhaps she actually chose Tom so he could protect her both against the world but also the self-destructive forces I am beginning to see that she contains within her.

In the same series of pictures autumn leaves are being gathered in a forest and there are a whole bunch of chestnuts into which they have probably stuck matches. They seem happy together.

The couple sitting a few aisles in front of me who are arguing could learn a thing or two from them. Stay home in Denmark, then, and give some attention to your grandchildren instead!. A trip to Latlandia never hurt anyone, in fact, it's a lot better than they say.

I scroll a little further down, searching around a bit.

She's friends with Milovan. That's something I would never have guessed. But she is. In some of his oldest profile pictures he has long hair gathered in a ponytail but now he's lost some of it and whatever is left has been cut short. With time, he has grown a little hollow-cheeked. At least I remember his somewhat elongated face as being fuller.

I hesitate for a moment, but then click on the small blue button and voila! I have sent a friend request to Milovan. And what made me do that? I don't even know myself, but I did, and now we'll just have to wait and see what he says.

I Wake Up When We Stop at Hellerup

I must have dozed off again. Both the couple and the man wearing the Icelandic sweater are no longer on the train. Funny how old couples always have to nag at each other.

I take out my telephone from my pocket. The digital clock on the top of the screen says that I need to be home in 32 minutes.

I go into the mail app and skim the mail from the principal once again because I'll actually already be leaving the day after tomorrow in order to be ready for Monday. Margrethe Harris is the principal's name and she knows how to make people feel good. She's bursting with a lively and contagious energy. I agreed to take the job in order to get a little bit away from everything and when I went there to speak with them in September it seemed like the perfectly right thing to do. But now I'm not so sure. You'll be teaching the Chinese students Danish, she explained. They don't celebrate Christmas and there are a whole lot of people on early retirement benefits and pensioners taking our shorter cultural courses for fun during the Christmas break, but you won't have much to do with them, Our "real teachers" will see to them.

A few days ago I spoke on the phone with the guy

with whom I'll be teaching the Chinese students, a school teacher from Gram. I have to admit that he makes me feel a bit uneasy. Back when the Chinese students arrived he gave them some rather heavy Danish names like Bitten, Tove, Frank, Torben and Gudrun. Sort of like on Ellis Island upon the immigrants' arrival to the US. It just makes everything so much easier, the Danish teacher explained to me, because Chinese names sound so alike.

Ying, Yang, Shing, Chang. It's no use letting them use those names because when they start talking about themselves then they get phonetically stuck in their delicate, light Chinese sounds which they won't ever be able to rid themselves of.

Get stuck? He also told me to be very careful about not letting them use the shared computers down in the cellar underneath the lecture hall. I had to assure him that I wouldn't or, he claimed, there would be nothing but Chinese characters everywhere which they wouldn't be able to remove from the computers and it would take ages to repair them, Some of them simply can't be repaired, he said, just so that I'd know. Okay, I'll keep that in mind, I reassured him. Yes, he said, and we've also had to take the key to the kitchen away from them. Why is that? Because they haven't made any effort to learn to appreciate good Danish food so when the rest of us are sleeping Bitten, Tove, Frank, Torben and Gudrun start making dumplings and black seaweed and other goodies from their home country. Well, in a way you can kind of understand that, I said. True, however, it's not so pleasant coming to a breakfast buffet the next morning that stinks of fried food. But luckily we're past all of that now and the locals no longer have to worry that their dogs might disappear and end up in a Chinese dish, he said laughing half-heartedly.

Twenty-five minutes. The train is still not moving. It's gonna be tight. I consider sending a text message to Lone that I might be delayed. Of course I could suggest that I instead pick up the kids at her place, at the posh apartment.

I'm not too eager to run into long-legged Morten who has been on the national team in both one category and the other. At least in the long jump and the triple jump.

It isn't really all that surprising if you think about it. If you've become really good at running fast and have been endowed with long legs, well then it's just a matter of flying across the sandbox once you're in the air. It's many years ago since he was active in the sport, but he's still got those legs meant for long-jump and that sporty fighter's spirit of his he's been able to convert to a solid career in the business world. I have no clue what his line of business is precisely. It's not a world I know anything about nor do I have any desire to preoccupy myself with it in any way, but it has provided him the means to purchase that extravagant apartment for Lone and the boys. You gotta give him that. Although in my opinion money isn't everything. There are other things in life, and the most joyful things come, I guess, in reality for free.

If I take a taxi from Copenhagen main station then I'll just be able to make it, I think. I can just afford that.

The money. I look at the empty seat next to me, the back pack. Where the hell is it? Well. It. Is. Not. There.

Fuck Fuck Fuck

I run as fast as I can along the train track on Hellerup Station, rush down the staircase in just a few steps, practically tumbling forward down inside the tunnel and skipping half a dozen steps as I do so, but I just manage it. I run across the tracks which the train, the breaks of which I can hear screeching above my head, will soon take me back to Hillerød and my backpack, which is most definitely still at that horrible winter-sausage-grill bar just waiting for me to come and get it. How dumb can a person be? How could I have forgotten it? It's utterly incomprehensible.

Getting to the train isn't so easy, there are throngs of people out Christmas shopping and taking their sweet time about it. But when I reach the staircase to track 1 things turn really bad because all the passengers who just got off the train I need to get on are now coming in hordes toward me. I push my way through but just when I reach the train track the train doors start sliding back shut. But I don't give up so easily, I pick up the pace and reach the train doors, try to force them open using all my strength. But they won't budge. I jump onto the narrow footboard and ride for a few meters before realizing the impossibility of my endeavor.

And I'm not the only one who does. The other nearby

passengers look at me with dismay as I rest my hands on my knees for a moment to catch my breath. And they continue to do so for a little too long a time, but they can stare all they want, I could care less. Nothing matters anymore now. I feel like giving a small boy the finger as his mother, who is wearing high-heel shoes and carrying a Wilson tennis bag on her shoulder, drags him along, but I make do with grimacing at him instead. I feel utterly ridiculous as I do it, but I've got to do something or other, don't I?

I look at the screen and can see that the next train, line B, will already be leaving in 6 minutes. Well, that at least works. I wonder if I should call them? Find the number to the grill bar and tell them I'm on my way?

No, probably not such a good idea to announce that I've forgotten a bag containing 175, 000 DKK somewhere below one of the tables. That would be really stupid.

I'll have to go up there and just hope for the best. I can be there in 20 minutes, give or take. It'll be fine.

Except for the fact that I won't be in my apartment when Lone rings my doorbell. I had better try to diffuse the situation as best I can so I write her a quick message saying that something urgent has come up but that I'm hurrying as much as I can. I add that I will pick up the boys instead, of course I will.

That's taken care of and now it's just a matter of remaining focused.

We're off to Hillerød. But first I just have to take a pee because that's something I've actually needed to do for a while now so I follow the signs to the back of the train station where you can park your bike and where the bathrooms are. But when I turn the corner I discover that the bathroom is occupied. The wide, green door is also completely covered in graffiti. It's probably no longer in use, in which case there must be some other bathrooms somewhere else. There can't only be one bathroom at Hellerup station, or what? This big cement hell of a place.

Well, it's gotta happen now. I look around. There is some low vegetation in a narrow bed and since there don't seem to be any people nearby there's nothing to worry about.

I stand with my legs apart, unzip my pants and send a long urinary stream into the bush, and without really knowing why I start rotating my hips, swinging everything that I can possibly swing and during this small moment, as I draw yellow circles in the snow, I feel truly happy.

I Open the Door to the Sausage Grill Bar

and walk in. I rush over to the spot where we had been sitting. There are hardly any people left. It smells like frying oil and wet dogs. It doesn't take long to establish the obvious: the backpack is, of course not here, Even though it's useless I start searching here and there just as one does when one is desperate. I even start moving some chairs around.

But, it dawns on me, did I, in fact, forget it here? Am I certain of that? I start thinking. No, actually, I'm not, because I may have had the backpack with me on the train, in which case it could have been the smoker wearing the Icelandic sweater who discreetly took it when he got off the train. That must have been in Birkerød.

Or what about the old couple with eczema on their lower legs because what do we really know about our fellow human beings when it comes down to it?

Well, now they'll certainly be able to afford their cultural travels to the big cities, beach vacations and numerous wonderful days at Latlandia.

What are you looking for? It is the young girl who earlier today was passing beers across the counter. She has braids, I now notice, with what resemble Christmas bells tied with red ribbon. It looks really stupid.

I tell her I'm looking for my backpack which I have forgotten here and can't seem to find.

What does it look like? She asks.

Blue, well, more like blackish blue, with lots of front and side pockets. It has a red handle. It's a Swiss brand: Victorinox.

With a white cross like the one that also makes Boy Scout knives?

No, I think those are Swiss Army knives, you mean. But that's not important. So you've found it?

She shakes her head.

Why the hell did you want to know what it looked like then?

Is she demented or what? I feel like pulling her Christmas-bell-braids, ding-dong, or at least saying something very unpleasant to her but don't get a chance to do any of those things before I hear her say that she's fairly certain that the woman I was talking with took it with her when she left.

Okay, well, that sounds good, but how do you actually know that?

I know because the woman both shouted and ran after you when you disappeared but she didn't get a chance to catch up with you because you were in a huge rush, it seemed.

I was, in fact, I had to catch a train.

She turns around and goes back to the sausage counter.

But thanks again, I say to her back.

She doesn't answer. If that's all it takes to insult her, well, that's her problem. It certainly isn't mine. My God.

I go back out into the cold weather which has gotten considerably colder.

I stand for a moment. Close my eyes. Take a deep breath.

This turned out good, I conclude. The envelope containing those gorgeous bills are, in other words, in the right hands.

And if you think about it, it is a rather natural course of events, isn't it? I mean, had I been the one who had run into an old acquaintance and the person had forgotten their bag, or shopping bags or Christmas presents, for that matter, then I would have taken care of those things, too. I mean, that's how we help our fellow humans. We take responsibility and the necessary action.

And that is a perfect example of how to get into the right Christmas spirit.

Yes, well, a small voice in the back of my mind starts to say, as I make my way to the train that will transport me back to Copenhagen, shouldn't Amina have contacted me by now? Wouldn't that be the most natural thing to do? Or what?

Well, that may be true, but she'll probably contact me any minute now, just you wait and see!

The Orange Race Bike

Morten Is, of Course, Also There

in the background with his long runner's legs. He is brimming with energy and is his usual annoying self. His glasses rest on the top of his head in his short, spiky hair. He is holding an iPad in his hand in the big open-plan kitchen. Lone goes back to the sofa where the boys can't tear themseleves from the TV screen. They are watching a family program on channel DR1. Right now one of the contestants has to make an estimated guess as to how many of the layer cakes that are hanging way up high a little fatso wearing a romper suit is able to topple while jumping up and down on a trapazee, to the great excitment both for the audience in the studio as well as for those watching at home from the couch, Rasmus and Casper press up close to their mother. Meanwhile, I am waiting in the hallway for my sons to come out. I want to take them home with me but it's as though they can't really pull themselvs together because they are determined to watch that fat idiot begin to jump, and I understand, because Morten is shouting something or other in the open kitchen that they are playing on an app which he is keeping an eye on on his iPad.

And while they are watching TV I look around and notice how nice their apartment is. And clean.

Which really shouldn't surprise me because as far as I remember Lone had a tendency to grab the vacuum cleaner at any random moment and start vacuuming. And when she was through with that she'd continue to the bathrooms which would get a thorough cleaning even if they didn't need it.

Yes, they live in a trendy, fashionable and designer-like home that, if anything, is perhaps a bit on the impersonal side, if not downright dull. The only thing that stands out is the orange Crescent racing bike which Morten has hung up on the long wall in the living room.

And yet not. Because isn't it, if you get right down to it, oh so predictably designer- retro-like? Yes, as a matter of fact, that's exactly what it is!

Finally the boys get to their feet when the clown in the romper suit as a kind of grande finale lies on the floor messing around in whipped cream and layer cake custard but they move with such reluctcance that even Lone feels sorry for me and that's almost the worst thing. I prefer it when she is angry and irritated with me.

She hasn't even asked me why I was delayed. It may very well be that she has, once and for all, given up on me, but we never were a good match for each other because whereas she would prefer things to go in a prefectly straight line I've always believed that there should be room for the more

skewed aspects of life that might take us new places as individuals. Like now, for example, where I'm going to Jutland to teach Chinese students.

I can still see Lone's face when I announced it a few months ago. What did you just say you are going to do?

They are starting to put on their jackets, the two boys, but then Rasmus just has to run to his room to get his sports bag.

Yes, he has to go to track and field tomorrow, I forgot to tell you, Lone says.

To what?

He's started going to track and field. The long jump and one hundred meters.

Oh, well, I'll say.

It's indoors, Lone says, as though that would make it sound better.

I'm about to come with a snide remark but decide against it.

I'm sure going to track and field is a good thing, I say instead.

She smiles and shuts her eyes for a moment.

Morten politely keeps himself in the background,

opens up a bottle of wine. The weekend is probably just starting for him.

Rasmus and Casper slip past me and out to the hallway.

Yes, come on boys, I think, let's rush off to the dark apartment on Kurlandsgade.

Should I Call

Amina now? Shouldn't she really have gotten in touch with me? As soon as we got back to the apratment and I had made the beds for the boys in the living room, I contacted her on Messenger. I wrote that it was very kind of her to take my bag for me, which is, in fact, a backpack, but that it was importnant that I got it back as soon as possible. I mentioned that it had been one of the Christmas girls that had stood behind the bar counter with Christmas bells in her hair who had been so kind as to inform me that she had seen the woman whom I had been sitting with take it. So I was in no doubt now that it had been her, Amina, who had it.

But that hasn't really been of much help because it is now 9:43 pm and the message was read over two hours ago. It would probably be a good idea to give her a quick call. I get out my phone and am just about to seearch for her number but end up holding it indecisiely in my hands. Should I or shouldn't I? Eeny, meeny, miny, moe.

Why do things always have to be so complicated? I've never been good at making these minor practical day-to-day decisions that still end up feeling so crucial when it comes down to it. And unfortunately life is full of them.

No, I finally conclude. It's late now and sending

another message wouldn't seem right, either. It's better to try to keep a slightly cool head and wait until tomorrow. There could be numerous, and for that matter very good, reasons why Amina hasn't replied. She may be at the movies with her husband, for example, or perhaps some friends have dropped by for a visit.

I don't know what her life looks like, or what has formed her. My impression is, now that I think about it, that she is a person who is easily influenced by others. No, there is more to it, she is a regular hanger-on, that's what she is. Period. There are those that might see that charateristic as a sign of openess, but I won't buy that. For example, after high school she had to go to Nepal all of a sudden for three months, because she happened to get a new friend, Dorte was her name, who, aside from building viking ships in Frederiksværk, also liked to trek. So Amina traveled with her to the other side of the planet and hiked up and down some beautiful mountains while letting her hair grow under her armpits and other places. That was apparently part of the travel package.

During our sophomore year there was a brief period in which folk music became her great interest so she harped away on a Balkan violin. It didn't sound good at all but she harped and harped away at the same time that she was high on a false sense of joy right until a friend of hers got her a job on the Hundested-Grenå ferry, then suddenly that was the big thing. Even though she had said earlier that she would never want to work on that ferry, who would? Well, apparently she did.

Once you first are able to see through it and notice it, then you see that she is a hanger-on in everything she has done. When earlier today I was looking at the picture of her and her husband and family I also got the impression that it was something they were pretending, almost like a real play. Look at us: we are out enjoying the autumn sun and look, now we are building a tree house for the kids together with their grandparents.

I actually don't understand how I could possibly have fallen so much in love with her as I truly did, but none of that matters because right now I basically just want to get my money back.

*

I hear a "bing" sound from the telephone and it vibrates as had it turned alive in my bare hands. When speaking of the sun it shines, I think, except it isn't shining a single bit because it's not from Amina but someone else. It is a message from my sister who writes that she has to speak with me. Things are really bad with Mom, she writes, with capital letters and exclamation marks.

Yes, well, I can imagine that she has reached new heights, is lying in the middle of her own vomit in the middle of the floor or runing around naked shouting at people on the common grounds.

I don't have the energy for it so I write that we'll have to wait and talk tomorrow because I finally managed to get my boys home with me. They are sitting here next to me, I lie, waving and sending their greetings. We should get together soon, I say, at least before Christmas. Good night and sleep well, Sis! We'll talk tomorrow. Everything is good.

I Place the Breakfast Roll

which I have just bought at the baker's on a big plate that I have taken out from the cabinet. I see now that it I may have overdone it but to be honest I just don't remember what the boys prefer and I don't want us to lack anything. At any rate, I've bought Mathilde Chocolate Milk and some pastry just like I did when I was married to Lone. I know for a fact that they like those things. It's very important to me that everything is as normal as possible during their stay with me, and what could be more normal than having bread from the bakery for breaksfast during the weekend?

See, athlete-Morten could learn a thing or two from that. The diet he was on when he was with the national team has now become their daily diet. It consists of quinoa, among other things, and a bunch of other dry kernels and seeds. There was also a day when Casper had a juice which, when I read the ingredients on the label, turned out to be made from "saved" fruit. They hadn't been picked but had fallen off the branches of their own accord, whereupon they were gathered and squeezed and then poured into botttles. Which sounds great and all but after I had had time to reflect on it it dawned on me just how stupid it was because what exactly was it that the fruit had been saved from? What about those ants and birds that had been cheated from a meal? It screams to high heaven of sheer idiocy, but our world has become full of examples like that and we'll just have to learn to live with and adjust to it and I am certain that Morten is one of those people who is excellent at just following the crowd, he's actually leading the way while the rest of us just make do with eating our Danish pastries and cakes and drinking our bitter coffee in sheer bitterness.

*

I have tried calling three times this morning but Amina hasn't answered. You can't exactly say that the collaboration is going well. Maybe she's slept late this morning, anyway, it's only 9 am. I have repeated on her answering machine that it is very important that I get that backpack because I actually need to go to Jutland tomorrow and I won't be returning until Jan 1st, so it's kind of a race against time.

The Boys Have Now Emerged at the Kitchen Door

They have both dressed which surprises me because they ususally aren't that keen on getting up early in the morning.

Well, gentlemen, have you slept well? I ask in an attempt to sound funny.

I actually need to leave now, says Casper.

What? Where are you going?

To track and field, he replies in a tone indicating that I should really have already been aware of that. And, yes, I can see that he's standing there with his sports bag and, yes, I was actually informed of it last night but I had, in fact, forgotten it and forgetting things is only human, afterall.

What about your breakfast?

Mom gave me some money so I'll just buy something on the way. There is something or other that's different about him. I can't figure out whether it's his hair, his clothes or what.

Where is it?

He looks at me perplexedly.

Track and field?

At Bellahøj Sports Center.

How will you get out there?

By bus, of course.

He has the same dejected tone as before, as though I don't have a proper grip on things. Which, in fact, I don't but I suddenly get the sense that Morten's arrogance has rubbed off on my oldest son. Which I really don't like. He'd better watch out with that, even though I can see that Lone and Morten's methods can give him the foundation he needs to grow into a strong young man, he still needs to watch the way he talks to his father. Because if he doesn't, where will that lead us?

Morten makes me feel safe, Lone said back when they had just met one another. At that point I thought that I was well on my way to winning her back but that wasn't the case at all. I could have continued pleading and begging, but first of all, that's not my style, and secondly, it wouldn't have helped. Lone is a strong and independent woman who has always known what she wanted and she wanted Morten.

He's also started getting long legs, Casper, which I suddenly notice when he walks out the door. He is only a few inches shorter than me now. I didn't have such long legs when I was thirteen. It's proabably all that "saved" fruit the birds and the ants should have had. It's almost as though his environemnt has imprinted itself on his body. It's sort of like when my mother advised me not to play basketball because everyone who played that "basket" game, as she called it, grew up to become long-legged bastards with big feet.

*

After Casper has left, Rasmus and I sit down to the enormous breakfast table I've set up. He doesn't want the pastry so I end up having to eat it all on my own.

Has he now also started getting ideas? One of my sons has started to sit down when he pees, like girls do, because last night I heard someone put the toilet seat up and down a couple of times when they went to the bathroom. In my family the men always stood up and my father even peed in the garden in the fishing house after it grew dark.

I tell Rasmus that I'm going to have to start packing a little because I'm going to the folk high school. He merely nods.

I explain to him that this morning the principal sent me a mesage saying that she'd like to see me partake in some mornign assemblies while I'm there.

I can tell by the look on his face that he doesn't know what a morning assembly is so I explain to him that

71

that is when you sing some of the good hymns from the Folk high School Song Book wherupon a mini-lecure is held on a thought-provoking, relevant topic which will give us something to think about right here and now and which will eventually make us more enlightened individuals in the long run.

But what else do you feel like doing today? I ask, since I can see that he isn't in the least interested in mornign assemblies.

I don't know.

We sit eating in silence for a lttle while.

How about a trip to Hundested when Casper returns? I ask.

In the Train on the Way to Hundested With the Boys

the extremely unpleasant dream I had last night suddenly re-emerges in my mind.

But in reality it might not be so unpleasant.

I was in a strange house in which a very confused cat was running around. It was as though it wanted to show me something so I followed it. It led me down a very dark hallway and to a room in which a doll with exceptionally long limbs was lying on the floor. It had to be removed, that doll. I don't know why, but I was determined to get rid of it. Maybe it was the cat that was influencing me, I don't know, but I started moving it. But it was hard because it was heavy and very stiff and unmanageable. Not until after I had been working on that annoying doll for a long period of time did it dawn on me that it was, of course, a dead version of Morten that I was trying to maneuver and apparently that realization was just what was needed because everything went much more smoothly after that. I threw it out the window. Yes, out the window with him, wehreupon I woke up and was in a totally fantastic frame of mind.

There Must Be Someone at Home

because the light is on and I think that I momentarilysaw a shadow moving around in the living room which disappeared into what must be the hallway.

I am standing by the fence gate together with the boys and looking up at Amina's house which resembles all the other houses on Lynæsbakken. Yellow brickstones, a covered terrace roof and a car port. I notice that they have two whole hothouses. And there is even a beehive in the backyard. Tom is probably the one who is preoccupied with tomaotes and insects and honey. He always was a big bear and as far as I remember Amina didn't exactly have green fingers but that doesn't man that she hasn't observed her husband and learned from him, also probably to show that she is also capable of growing plants, etc.,—look I can, too! And I'll also venture a guess that they probably have a hothouse each where she can can peek all the time at whatever at whatever he's growing in his.

Why are we here? Rasmus asks.

I already told you.

Neither of the boys were all too eager to spend their Saturday going to Hundested but we left anyway as soon as Casper returned from track and field. I lured them by saying we'd go to Knud Rasmussen's House, but that was quickly over and done with and it was, to be honest, a bit of a disappointment. It was, of course, interesting, with all those fantastic adventures he had experienced on those crazy expeditions in the Arctic regions and the house itself with the walrus teeth, seal skins and tupilaks and even a kajak that was hanging from the ceiling was fairly exciting to explore at the same time that it was a little strange that all these things that originated in wide and expansive spaces had been crammed into this single small white-washed home.

Neither Casper nor Rassmus seemed all too impressed.

At the same time, I really don't think there is any need for the boys to be so negative because we also went to the City Bakery where they got a hot chocolate and a sandwhich roll.

This was where the old Waffel Corner used to be and I got this sudden urge to see it now that we were here anyway. It's gotten totally renovated, among other things, it's been expanded and now includes the space of a clothes shop that used to be next door to it. At any rate, it was on these premises that Amina pulled down her pants and let the owner give her a proper spanking. The images of what happened are constantly on my mind. I can't get rid of them. I imagine the owner had bushy eyebrows.

The conversation we had at the grillbar has, somehow, made a deep impression on me.

Afterward I told the boys that I just needed to pick something up from someone I know and that's why we are now standing here. I open the gate to the yard and walk up the tiled pathway leading to the front door.

Casper and Rasmus politely follow behind me because they have also understood that laser tag and pizza are on the agenda later today at Laserdoom in Hillerød on our way home. It's not something we've ever tried before but I think they have the perfect age for it now and it would be stupid to wait any longer if it's ever going to happen. I've told them it's a little like playing cops and robbers.

I press the doorbell, a small classical-looking thing-a-majig on the door panel, but it doesn't seem like there's any repsonse in there. I wait a moment and then I knock on the door with my fists.

I place my ear on the door. I think I can hear somethign in there, some light, quick steps, like someone is approaching, very good, I just manage to think before a violent, deep barking begins, and I jump back in fear.

Damn! Through the frosted glass of the window I see the silhouette of a dog that runs along the right side of the door. The glass window isn't hazy all the way to the top, so the big brown-black head of the dog becomes visible as the big creature jumps up and down.

God, it's ugly. Well, at least it's stopped barking but makes do with growling every time it lands to catch its breath. I think it might be a Rottweiler which are known for being espeically dangerous and unpredictable.

If anyone's at home they must have heard this, but there is still no response.

Maybe we should just leave? Rasmus says.

I know that he isn't crazy about dogs. He even stays away from my mother's harmless Scottish terrier. He pretends to greet the dog whenever we go over there, without doing it at all.

Okay, I say when it becomes pretty clear that there isn't much more I can do.

We start walking down the garden path, but before we reach the fence I stop.

Wait here, I say and start to jog back to the house. I skip the tiles by the front door and go around to the backyard, I don't want to risk having to go all the way back to Copenhagen if it turns out that someone was home afterall. That would be really silly.

I peer into the living room that is dominated by heavy pieces of furniture in black leather. I cup my face with both hands so I can better focus through the window. The interior is actually rather Balkan-like, multi-colored and somewhat bombastic, a littlel like her parents' home back in the day. Lots of trinkets and knick-knacks. Heavy curtains.

She has a small Italian flag on the wall, I notice. Well, I'll say. Seems she's perpetuating her father's big lie.

I continue to the first of three rooms that are situated in a row. It must be the bathroom because there is ventilation and the same kind of opaque glass window as at the front door. Then I reach what must be the parents' bedroom. There is family photo both on the wall and on the nighttable. One of the walls has a rose-pink color and there is a landscape picture of southern Europe hanging on it.

And there it is again, by god, that ugly Rottweiler in the middle of the room. It is salivating as it looks up at me with its big head cocked to the side. Despite the fact that it is horrendously ugly it looks rather harmless.

I'm just about to leave when I catch sight of my backpack. It is standing on the floor together with the three filled-up Christmas present shopping bags Amina had had with her at the shitty sausage grillbar. It looks like she just threw everything on the floor and left it there because she was in a rush to go somewhere else.

Okay, I think, so that's where it is.

I'm just about to leave when I siddenly catch sight of one of the neighbors, an older man, behind the fence. He is standing in his living room and I pretend to be checking something in the beehive, taking my time as I do so.

The boys are already standing on the street waiting for me as I emerge from the other end of the house.

Come on, we're going home, I say, walking toward the center of town.

They slowly follow behind me.

Weren't we going to play laser games?

We'll have to see, I say.

You Can Actually See the Water Here from Lynæsbakken

And the ferry. It is it at bay. I think the route has been shhut down.

I wonder if it's the same ferry that Amina worked on back in the day?

You never know, but what I do know is that when I picked her up from the ferry on one windy afternoon she had a big hickey on her throat. She had lifted the collar of her jacket a little up toward her ears, but I noticed it immediately. I can conjure forth every tiny miserbale detail if I had to. There was a crest of foam on the water in the dock, unlike today which is calm and Amina was standing there with her hair all dishevelled which she couldn't straighten out. She seemed upset and told me that she had been pressed up against the wall by a colleague who was the one who had done it. Just like that. Sucked on her throat. Against her will, of course.

She had been holding a big baking sheet filled with hotdogs that were so popular among the pasengers so she was unable to protect herself from the culprit.

What a jerk, I said.

Yes, she too thought it had been extremely unpleasant.

I couldn't get it out of my mind back then so I used to come and stand on the ferry berth when Amina got off work. Then I'd stand and stare up at the spot on the boat where her colleagues used to go ashore and tried to figure out which one it could have been.

At first I kept my eyes on a cook apprentice who had long hair underneath his chef's cap and then an engineer.

The chef's apprentice seemed genuinley surprised when I confronetd him and the only thing he could somewhat cryptically say was that you never really could tell for sure what Amina was up to.

I suggested she go to management and not just put up with it.

Well, she didn't want to do that, but she didn't want to come out with who it was who did it, all she wanted was to forget all about it.

You have no choice, I said, to report it and also tell me who it was.

But none of those things ever happened even though she had promised me she would do them, and you are supposed to keep your promises. Okay, we are now on our way to the laser games.

Laserdoom Has Locations with Exciting Courses All Over the Country

it says on a sign which continues: where an enthusiastic and experienced instructor is always ready to instruct and advise you so the pace will be upbeat and high throughout the entire event.

My mood hasn't improved especially, and I don't find Laser Lars, as the instructor is called, all too impressive. He is wearing braces and is speaking in such a low voice that I can barely hear what he is saying. But it doesn't really matter because the basic idea is to aim at your opponent and peg away, how hard can that be? Just let us onto the course so we can get started! We've all chosen a laser pistol and put on the equipment so how long do we have to wait on this ante-room?

I don't know how to interpret the fact that Amina wasn't at home but no matter what there is no reasonable explanation for her not getting back to me. On the other hand, it has now been properly established that she has the backpack, at last I learned that much from my visit and I have made sure that she knows that I know that she has it.

My telephone is now vibrating audibly in my pocket whereupon Laser Lars sends me a very strict look which I in a way can understand because our telephones are supposed to be either on airplane- mode or completely switched off but I'm going to have to take this one call, which I indicate to him by pointing my finger up in the air.

But I could have saved myself the trouble because it's just my sister. I whisper into the phone that it's not a good time right now but before I get a chance to hang up I register something or other about my mother and a parquet floor. Whatever the hell that's supposed to mean.

But we'll have to talk about all of that later because right now they are opening the two doors that resemble something from a spaceship on each side of the room, finally, the games can begin.

I follow the other blue members of my team into a huge room that makes up the course itself. Rasmus and Casper have ended up on the red team.

It's really dark in here. Perhaps more than it should be. All I can basically see are the blue shining punks on my team members' outfits as we make our way to the start position we've been assigned. Everything is made of wood and in many of the walls there are holes through which you can see and shoot. It is a labyrinth on several levels. That's not bad. Perhaps it's actually even better than the one at Holbæk Go-cart course. I used to go to as a teenager. Those were the days. We'd usually fill up two cars and would drive down there divided in the two teams that were going to play against each other and we'd use the drive to plan our strategy. We were really into it back then.

Someone or other shouts that we have to stick together, but it seems to me that our team has spread out rather quickly. The equipment is heavy and I can feel that I'm beginning to sweat.

I suddenly get the feeling that I am alone, but that's actually okay, I prefer it that way. I start to creep around, keeping an eye on those red bastards we're supposed to kill because I am really starting to get gripped by the mood, my adrenalin is starting to pump.

It's not long before a shadow emerges before me with the signature red goal areas indicated on his outfit and I shoot him without hesitation—bang! You're dead, and besides the small clicking sounds from my trigger there is an electronic downward sound indicating that I hit bull's eye and that an electronic life has now been taken. It's not long before more antagonistic red devils show up who were lured here by the shooting sounds, but I quickly retreat, backing further and further away, wait and then shoot another round. At least two die and the rest run for their lives. That'll teach 'em! And imagine how dead they would have been if it had been for real because then their blood would have been flowing along with their intestines in the hallways, it would have been a veritable massacre.

Then I change tactics, also because I need to catch my breath, take a small break. I crawl up ito soemthing that resembles a watch tower, squat down and peer out through the holes. I can really get a proper view of the course from here and I see a bunch of red and blue lights moving around down there. I catch sight of two shadows whom I recognize as Casper and Rasmus. They have apparently chosen to stick close together and now they are approaching my watch tower. I remain sitting completely still, wait until they are just below me in an open space, wherupon I get up in a single movement and shoot a short round which immediately kills them both. And then I duck back down.

Through one of the peepholes I observe them as they remain standing looking around in confusion like two broken red light bulbs. Run to safety, you two idiots! But they don't, so as soon as their equipment is up and running I pop up again, sending a new shower of laser light which should properly kill them this time.

They have now caught sight of me.

They look at their father in disbeleif.

Well, what did you two think? It's a matter of winning, isn't it? Get in the game, already!

Are You Ready for the Bad News?

my sister asks on the telephone. We are back in the ante-room, taking off our vests and weapons. No, actually I'm not. I wipe off the sweat from my forehead with a napkin. I sense that my pulse is starting to go back down. I feel really great.

It's Mom, my sister says.

Yes, I was able to gather that. What's up with her?

She's come to regret it. It's a terrible mess.

I sense that I am irritated by the fact that my sister always has to be so long-winded. She is never able to just say what's on her mind. So I keep quiet until she continues on her own and I manage to take a grooved plastic cup and pour a little of the free coffee into it before she finally collects herself and tells me that our mother has reached the conclusion that she doesn't want to give the money to us afterall. From what I gather from my sister, the fact that she had agreed to give them to us has pulled her out of the black hole she was in. She has managed to reach the light. That is the image my sister uses because mom had been out running, I mean, she had been out for an actual run, wearing a pair of new, colorful jogging shoes while dragging her utterly confused dog behind her on a leash. I can just picture it. When my sister had visited her later that day my mother was busy taking down the wallpaper in the bedroom and she had said that now was the time, there were a lot of changes that were going to have to be made and those changes were going to cost money. And since we had been keeping her money for her, the time had come to return it.

My sons are standing a little ways from me discussing the results of the game that have just appeared on the scoreboard. They talk about who Knud could be because he is the one who has, unrivalled, scored the most points. A little simple arithmetic tells you that he single-handedly has managed to make no less than 34 direct hits.

I am the one who is Knud because that was the warrior name I chose when we signed up to Laserdoom and just like the great Polar explorer I, too, have a calling for I am also about to embark on a journey across the ice cap in a mind-blowingly minus fourty degree temperature weather and I am certain that I'll be able to manage it.

Are you still there? My sister asks.

Yes, of course.

There is a pause.

She also wants a new parquet floor in the living room.

A new floor?

Yes, and from what I can surmise, she has already called in the carpenters and they started work on it this morning.

Casper Used to Always Order Hawaii Pizza

but today he has chosesn a vegetarian pizza and, unsurprisingly, as soon as it comes it is apparent that that was not a good choice because it looks really slushy and unappetizing.

He stares at it for a long time.

Doesn't look too great, I say.

He shrugs his shoulders, mentions something about organic tomatoes and starts eating with a hearty appetite as I sit watching him.

Eat properly, young man! I allmost feel compelled to say, because he's immediately gotten yellow cheese and green spinach around his mouth. He just stuffs it into his moouth with his fork which easily penetrates the soft lasagna pasta. He doesn't use his knife at all. Just lets it lie there on the table.

But I mnage to compose myself. I point at one of the loud yellow signs indicating that we are at Amager Pizza Place and I take my time to explain to both of them that at this particular place, which the name already implies, you eat pizza. Just like you wouldn't order an entrecote at a fish restaurant and at Jensen's Bøfhus you would steer clear of the flounder. It's important knowledge to share and while they are pondering over that I glance at an email that has just clicked in to my inbox from

Margeret Harris which, to be honest, is making me slightly uneasy.

Once more she writes how much they are looking forward to my presence at the folk high school and that's when it comes: Since your major is History it might be a nice opportunity for you to introduce yourself by giving a lecture or two in the short culture course which will also run through Christmas together with the Danish course. We would like to take full advantage of our teachers' expertise so as to ensure that our students get as much out of their stay as possible.

I'm not too crazy about that idea, and I can't say that I particularly care for her tone, either.

We eat in silence for a little while. Incredible how much they are clittering and clanking the plates and dishes behind the counter.

I take out my phone and write back to Margrerhe Harris that I will think about it.

I Finally Hear From Amina

which happens while we are walking down Amagerbrogade on our way back home to the apartment. She writes on Messenger that she'll call back in a half hour, if that's okay with me.

Absolutely, I write back cheerfully.

When we get into the apartment the boys hurl themselves at a computer game in the living room. They ask whether I want to join them but I'm not really in the mood and anyway, perhaps I've beaten them enough times for one day.

Instead I go into the bedroom and start putting clothes, socks, pants, underwear, shirts and sweaters into a big suitcase. I don't really have to take all that much with me, the folk high school has a laundromat. The folk high school is a little like a summer camp with its scent of the old days. I had actually planned that I would spend some time now packing and envisioning what my life is going to be like in Jutland but I don't because the only thing I can think about right now is when will Amina pull herself together to call me? When I close my suitcase, which is much too full, thirty-five minutes have passed. I go out into the kitchen and skim though some papers and bills that I have been pinned to the wall. I take a beer from the fridge, open the can and take two sips. I notice that Casper and Rasmus who are sitting on the sofa in the little room are watching me. No, I still don't want to play any games with you, if that's what you guys are after. You'll have to entertain yourselves.

I take my beer with me over to the window.

Fourty-two minutes.

I look out at the courtyard where large areas have been blocked off because some of the co-op's facades have to be repaired. The work will begin in January, as I just read in one of the many papers I have taken a quick look at, and it's going to continue for the next many weeks. They are going to set up a scaffolding and the building will be wrapped in plastic and the carpenters will begin their noisy business from 7 am in the morning. We don't want to have to put up with that, the boys have announced, so they'll be staying with their mother during those weeks. I have a sneaking suspicion it's really so that they can uninhibitedly crawl up onto the couch to Lone and Morten and watch family programs on Danish TV.

Aside from that, I just remembered that I really need to have a serious talk with Casper. Even though he shouldn't consider the fact that he came in last at today's games as a huge failure , he shouldn't start coming up with all kinds of dumb excuses as to why he didn't do better. I heard him say something about his laser pistol not working properly, something which he's got to stop doing.

Maybe it's something he's picked up from Morten? Who knows? Maybe it's that tall, long-legged bastard I'll have to confer with.

*

The kitchen is suddenly filled with a jingling tone coming from my telephone.

Finally! It's Amina.

Hi, she says.

It was nice seeing you.

Nice seeing you, too.

How's it going?

Fine.

I'm sorry for not getting back to you earlier.

That's okay, I say, even though I don't mean it.

I'm in England.

In England?

Yes, together with Tom. His parents are watching the kids.

In Ringsted? I hear myself ask which I immediately regret because it gives away the fact that I have checked her out on social media. In which case, I better not ask her who is babysitting the dog who it sounds like is home alone.

What are you doing in London? I pull myself together and ask.

It's actually a kind of tradition Tom and I have, we go to London for a short breather before all the Christmas madness starts.

I see. That does sound cozy.

I'm waiting at the reception. Tom is just taking a quick bath before we go out for dinner.

She almost sounds cheerful.

Well, good for you, I think.

When will you be back?

Monday, it's a prolonged weekend, isn't it?

But there's just the issue with my backpack, I'm leaving for Jutland tomorrow and won't be back for the next few weeks.

She, of course, wants to know what I'm going to be doing in Jutland and so I explain it to her.

That sounds exciting, but can't I just send the backpack to you in Jutland? she asks.

I consider her suggestion for a moment but decide that I don't have the wherewithal for that. I know that it's not everything that gets lost in the mail, but some things do and my nerves just wouldn't be able to take having to wait for it and just hoping for the best.

No, that's okay. You know what we'll do?

No.

I'll try to see if I can get away from the folk high school next Saturday and then I'll come to Hundested and pick it up from you, if that's okay?

But are you really going to make that long journey there? It'll be the night before Christmas Eve?

I can hear some of the hotel guests speaking in a foreign language in the background. I can surmise that she is having something to drink because she moved her mouth from the receiver for a moment. I imagine she is sitting in a fancy dress in the lobby with a glass of wine waiting for her husband.

You bet I do. I also have to pay a visit to my mother, so it's no problem.

She mentions something or other about how she hopes I don't rush out the door in a panic like last time.

Ha ha ha, I laugh, no, of course not.

I explain to her that I had to pick up my two boys at Lone and her new husband's place and it had been so cozy seeing Amina and the time had simply flown by and I didn't want Casper and Rasmus to have to wait for their father to show up.

That's not how it should be.

I understand, and that's very commendable of you and. she asks whether I managed it in time.

Managed what?

To pick up the boys, of course.

Yeah...I say hesitantly.

Well, that's good.

Yes, and we had a nice calm Saturday here at home playing video games and eating pizzas, Everything's been just fine.

I still regret having mentioned Ringsted before.

Well, that sounds very nice.

Pause.

You are giving me a bit of a guilty conscience, she says, sitting here without the kids. We were actually considering whether we should bring them along next year now that they are a little bigger but I'm still in doubt as to how much they'd get out of it.

A new pause.

Or maybe that's just something we say to give us more adult time alone, but anyway, I'm looking forward to seeing you again.

Me too, I say.

I think we are about to conclude the conversation, but apparently we aren't because she is now adding that she is so pleased with the fact that we could confide in one another the way we did, to such a degree, in fact, that she hasn't been able to bring herself to tell Tom about it.

Oh, well...

But it's still strange, isn't it, that it felt as natural as it did?

I don't know what to say, but it seems that Teddy Bear Tom, who apparently doesn't know his wife ran into me in Hillerød, is taking his sweet time in the shower.

I mean, after not having seen each other for so many years.

How can she go on like that? I wonder, knowing I ought to respond with something or other but before I get a chance she starts talking again.

She tells me that she already knew back then, in fact, at the very same moment that she got into Milovan's car, that she was making a big mistake and that she of course shouldn't have gone with him to that gravel pit when we she and I were going steady and all, and it was totally out of proportion considering how much older he was, but what does one know at that age? She hopes I'm not angry with her after all these years.

Got into Milovan's car? I say and can sense a sizzling feeling in my abdomen. What the hell is she talking about?

It's as though there's a big revolving stage that starts moving in my mind and all the events connected with the famous birthday are spinning along with it because none of what I thought had happened matches up any longer. I was aware of the fact that more things had taken place, but she can't possibly be telling me that she went with her uncle to a gravel pit on her own free will? She could have just have said no.

But apparently she didn't.

I Am Still Trembling

when the next day I am sitting on the train on my way to Jutland—I would even say it's increased in strength. It turns out that there was a reason for why Amina had gone with Milovan to Ølsted Gravel Pit in the beautiful weather. She was going to be photographed in a handball t-shirt which he had helped design. Besides being in charge of the vegetable department in Bilka he was also an amateur photographer and handball trainer for B70 Taastrup. Why it had to be a place with bulldozers, piles of stone and noisy industrial machines, remains unknown, but that's at least what Amina told me before Tom showed up in the lobby. With wet hair, I was just about to add.

It's crazy to think about, because I was just lolling around like an untrained puppy, never crossing the line with my young girlfriend. But Milovan did, on the other hand. He probably really gave it to her in the gravel pit. On the other hand, it' so long ago that it really shouldn't play a role anymore, but it does and I'm thinking back on it with very antagonist feelings, I must say.

She never told me anything about it, and ever since yesterday I have been racking my brain to recall   the events from back then. Did she seem sad the following days after her birthday? Not as far as I remember. It was a pretty busy period in her life. I know. She had just gotten a job on the ferry.

Through the window I look out at the Denmark we are passing through. We will soon be in Korsør. At 6:32 pm we will be in Vejen where the school caretaker will pick me up. You can expect a hot meal waiting for you when you arrive, the principal had written. The implicit message being: that's how we do things around here. We look out for each other.

But I couldn't give a screw about the breaded pork patties with organic potatoes which, I understand, have been put aside for me, because if I dig deep down there is still a lot of crap waiting to pour out from back then, which I didn't know I still contained. Take for example the summer day when I biked to Liseleje with Asger. I remember it clearly. We struck up a conversation with Amina and her friend. They were sunbathing topless amongst the dunes. They were both very cute, but Amina was especially. She was totally irresistible, while there was something oddly unfinished and gangly about the other girl which I didn't like. She also had very light hair which was a little thin at the ends.

We went to get ice cream, Asger and me, because I have always had this affinity for ice cream and that way they wouldn't have to put their tops back on. They should be allowed to remain lying there and get nice tans, after all, there are so few hours of sunshine in Denmark. When we returned with ice cream cones and candy the girls, somewhat upset, told us that some Milovan-types and dog-walkers had swarmed about them. Asger and I immediately agreed that that was really disgusting. After all, why shouldn't the girls be allowed to lie topless on the beach in peace, the most natural of all natural activities to do in the world?

We had a wonderful day at the beach and when we had to go home, the breasts were packed away, no more sun for today, the four of us walked together through the narrow path of spruce trees that is most probably still there between the beach and Liselejvej.

And I clearly remember that Amina was struggling to wheel her bicycle through the forest floor because it was all sandy. It was some shifting sand which the wind had flown in from the beach. The rest of us had parked our bikes by the roadside but her bike was completely new so she didn't want to risk doing that. At any rate, I let myself fall behind together with her and as we were approaching the road I said outright that I would like to quickly see her breasts. Just one last time.

I also said, when I noticed that she hesitated slightly, that it couldn't make all that much difference to her whether I saw them on the beach or in the forest. What difference could that possibly make?

Did I really say that? That sounds completely inappropriate, in fact, it doesn't sound right to me that I ever said anything like that.

Yes, well, you did, because the dog-walker and Milovan weren't there and that sort of thing doesn't just go away just because you can't admit it, does it? You can't run away from the fact that you are who you are.

However didn't she allow herself to fall behind on purpose, suddenly placing herself in a vulnerable position which I couldn't help taking advantage of?

Yes, maybe she did, in the end, go along with it, but perhaps she just got so tired of your nagging that she simply remained standing, holding both hands on the handlebar as you unbuttoned her shirt, because she was wearing one of those, you recall, and she let you see what you wanted to, there were a few grains of sand on her moist skin, but that, of course, wasn't enough, was it?

Perhaps not.

No, because the more you get the more you want, so you started tweezing and touching a little and toying again, and it was so incredibly good that you'll never ever forget it so it's not so hard to imagine how Milovan felt on the day when he drove off with Amina and his great big camera lying in the backseat.

That's By the Way True.

Milovan played tennis with Amina's father, in the brown pavilions up in the forest of Hundested.

I went there together with Amina a few times and they really went at it, I can tell you. The ceiling was actually too low for tennis in the old premises. The court wasn't suitable for Amina's father's soft, slicy style. He could forget all about scoring love. On the other hand, it suited Milovan's aggressive and more direct style. As I recall it, he had a backhand that wasn't to be sneezed at which he sent hard down the line with no mercy.

Life at the Folk High School

I am standing by the steps

to the main building observing a small group of Chinese people making their way across the courtyard as they speak Chinese. They disappear into the library and I see the light switch on in the classroom which I know smells of chalk because they still use chalks and chalkboards in there. All they are waiting for now is for me to come and start the day's lesson. But I remain standing on the steps just a little while longer because it is my third day and I already feel like I am suffocating. It's really not so much because of my Chinese students because they keep mostly to themselves and are very careful with everything. It's more those enthusiastic retirees and students on early retirement benefits that are a real burden. They are everywhere, at least that's what it feels like; they shuffle around in the hallways in their slippers, sit around reading newspapers in the TV room. They have opinions about and take a stance on everything they encounter and they give out clear signals at every chance they get that the teaching material presented to them contains information they already know and if they didn't know it beforehand it wasn't worth knowing in the first place. They would, in fact, much rather listen to themselves. Their wrinkled mouths only stop moving when they are stuffing themselves with cake. Fortunately, there is an awful lot of cake, remember, we are in southern Jutland, and there is usually also always a little something sweet served after dinner.

But all that cake isn't good for them because all their lives they have both had their cake and eaten it, too. They have been so exceedingly spoiled and privileged to an inconceivable degree because already back in the day when these retirees were young it was all plain sailing, they could choose to study whatever they wanted. And as soon as they had they finished their damn degree there were millions of jobs waiting for them.

Of course, austerity measures galore, but when the bad times turned good they had it easy with cheap bank loans and steady jobs and then they just continued on that way until they turned sixty where the new early pension was waiting or them. Talk about having an easy time of it.

And it doesn't even stop there, because just when those spoiled early retirees had started being sexually active when the birth control pill hit the market and it was the era of non-stop parties and frolicking and later when they grew mature in years the medicine industry came up with that little blue pill to keep things lively and now I had better go to my class because I can see

Chinese shadows staggering around in the classroom.

But what are you all really doing here? Out in the middle of this hill-billy country, as far away from home as you can possibly get. Yes, I realize that in another part of the world there is still a boom which makes the happy youth of the early retires look like, well, nothing, because from what I understand half of the world's cranes are to be found where my Chinese students derive from and while those cranes are lifting whatever it is they lift, hundreds of thousands of Chinese have left China to travel the world and ten or twelve of you have now, for reasons that are unknown, ended up here in Rødding, and when I look into your eyes I see, what shall I say, a slightly dull look in them, but, that's beside the point, Let's just start so we can get those wonderful Danish verbs out of the way.

At First I Didn't Hear Anything from Amina

but the last few days she has been flooding me with little implicit greetings, like now, where I am on my way to the first coffee break of the day. She has sent a photo, I now see, in which you can see white frost on a branch outside of her window. Very interesting, If I look closer I notice it must have been taken from her bedroom because a little bit of her clothes closet is in the picture. It feels a little forbidden, the fact that I know how she lives without her really knowing that I know. I respond with a quick smiley because under current circumstances it's just a matter of keeping the channels wide open. I continue toward the main building where I can hear music playing from an open window. Is that Bon Jovi? Jesus, who listens to that these days?

When I enter the dining hall it is already filled with pensioners even though I finished class ten minutes to the hour. I rush to the closest of the three tables with thermo-pots and of course don't manage to pour more than half a cup of coffee, which is of the same standard as my parents' from Aldi, before Birger-Bo shows up and is clearly seeking contact. I try to avoid him and try to seem very preoccupied with the freshly baked roll on which I am smearing butter but he still manages to invade my private space.

"Hi!" he says, as he catches my eye and remains standing on his new hips which were bought and paid for at Hamlet Private Hospital, whereupon he proceeds doing the thing with the palm of his hand, where he rubs his stomach, a stupid habit of his which is both embarrassing and unsuitable at the same time.

Today he wants to hear a little bit about the bus trip to Flensborg because a two-day trip to Flensborg has been arranged in the belief that it will create a better sense of shared community between the pensioners and the Chinese students who tend not to socialize with one another. He especially wants to know about the historical aspects of the trip which he expects there will be quite a bit of, and since we both majored in history I must be the right one to ask, or what?

You would think so, I admit, but I can't explain the program because I'm not the one who has arranged it. Furthermore, as he probably can understand, it was all planned way before I started at Rødding, so unfortunately I can't help him.

It's as though he doesn't really listen to what I'm saying. He starts blabbering away about the Isted-Lion and the refined raw rum that was brought to Flensborg from the West Indies.

I intend to get a taste of Danish colonial history

while we're there anyway. I can hear that he's already read up on it and feels a great need to share that information. Perhaps he should instead keep a better eye on his wife who has grown increasingly popular amongst the other older gentlemen. I don't know what it is about pensioners, but sometimes they behave like they're back in eighth grade.

You'll have to excuse me, I say, and am about to leave because I simply can't stand listening to that braggadocio any longer. At that very moment the principal shows up and asks if I am all settled in now.

I nod.

She is wearing an elf hat and emitting the scent of an expensive perfume that neither matches her outfit nor the countryside environment we are in, but she smells good. I like her, she has a charming way with people.

She asked whether I recalled that we had spoken about what I could contribute with on the culture course. I may be able to, I answer.

Birger-Bo smiles with interest.

I add that I'll be sure to come up with something, it's all under control, make no mistake about that.

But then perhaps you could do it quickly, Harris, says, because on Saturday evening, little Christmas Eve, there is an empty spot in the program which would be nice to be able to fill out. So it's just a matter of getting started.

It's clear that I am expected to present something, because that's what you do at a Folk high School. You make a presentation. I can hear that I sound a little uncooperative, but that is because I am realizing that I will have to forget all about my little trip to Hundested.

Well, if you need an answer right here and now I might as well give it to you, I say, so as not to lose the initiative entirely. It's a lost case, anyway.

Birger-Bo looks at me expectantly, his hand beginning to rub his stomach.

Knud, I hear myself say.

Knud?

Yes. Knud Rasmussen and his great sleigh journey. That's what I'm going to talk about.

I sense that as soon as I say it I realize that it's an idea I've had for quite a while and which has now worked it's way through as a manifestation. It feels totally right.

And give me the entire afternoon, then. Give me all the time that needs to be filled out.

I Climb the Stairs

in the left wing of the building for on the very top the library annex is certain to have books on both the Great Sleigh Ride and a couple of Knud's dairies.

My steps make an echo and for every floor I climb I can see through the small square-shaped windows across the brown-fogged landscape with the ploughed fields, edged with hedges and a few bare trees. A few farms. And I can, of course, see the church located just next to it.

I can sense that I am beginning to sweat. But it's not mere perspiration, because it's getting colder and colder the higher up I get, probably because the insulation in the tower walls is poor, who knows? But never mind about that, because it's nothing compared to the cold Knud had to endure because he was no quitter, he did what had to be done and I'm now going to get started on what needs to be done and read about his great accomplishments, yes indeed, the lonely sleigh rides with the barking dogs running at the front of it and pulling you into a darkness that is unknown. And there'll definitely be time to look into all that wife-swapping that took place in the igloos because when the fish oil lamp was blown you can bet that the bag of genes was properly shaken and so not too many cross-eyed and semi-idiots were born. They probably all smelled of fish oil. Because it practically seeped out of their skin, the Inuits, just think of all the fresh seal and whale blubber they consumed all day.

The little and cold library with its old, worn-out books is situated in the dark, here, but then I catch sight of Elvira Hattensen, Birger-Bo's wife, who is smoking behind the gym.

Isn't it her? It's hard to see through these windows because they don't exactly get cleaned every day up here.

Yes, indeed, it is her and I've noticed that she steps out and has a cigarette every now and then. I'm sure that Birger-Bo isn't too crazy about it, that little bad habit of hers, are you, Birger? Because you're always boasting about how you stopped smoking from one day to the next, when was it? Back in 1992? And ever since you have exuded that impudent holier-than-thou attitude you only find in former smokers.

But Elvira Hattensen is standing down there smoking despite all that, which serves you well, you show-off. And she should just continue doing it, because what you don't know won't hurt you and according to your own account, Birger, you met each other in elementary school and even though you claim to have known right away that you were meant for each other I must admit that I find that a little hard to believe. I think that your NARRATIVE is a big fat lie, Birger-Bo. One can sense that sort of thing. I think the truth is that you were a smooth-talking charmer, but that she very soon discovered just how big a drag you really are, but she somehow managed to put up with it, time passed and soon the whole menagerie had lasted, well, nearly a lifetime. Apparently, you couldn't have children, What exactly do you do, Birger-Bo spray with bog-water, or what? Perhaps you should have played the Eskimo's little lamp game, but that didn't come to much, did it? So now all you're left with are theater trips, cultural travels and stays at folk high schools.

Meanwhile you are terribly preoccupied with how others are doing and how they live their lives because you love to snoop into other people's business so you can judge them, but we'll leave it that for now because that's a bit of a touchy a subject.

Now she's started to pace back and forth, down there, Elvira, and it is in that delicate, light and feminine way because she doesn't yet have those stiff, brand-new Birger-Bo hips that the body hasn't quite come to terms with yet. Oh, no, she has soft movements that almost, but only just almost, might resemble that of a young girl.

You Can See It All From Up Here,

not only the church but also the waterworks and the butcher and the country road that twists and turns through the landscape to the neighboring town, whatever it is called.

Right now Malte Fagtman is playing soccer with my Chinese students on the handball court even though it is wintry cold and windy outside. Malte, who has taken out his old soccer shoes. is really into it. And boy, are they getting some tackling done! The Chinese students are running around and laughing and having a great time and, of course, don't really have any idea what the point of the whole thing is.

Malte is from the area, Rødding, and is a former cabinet maker of the old school and as far as I understand, he's worked for Fritz Hansen himself. He is a smart enough guy, but his brain is deteriorating, He suffers from slight dementia and sometimes stops talking in the middle of a sentence and often forgets what he is doing.

Like right now, where he is standing down there looking like he doesn't quite know why he is holding a soccer ball or surrounded by a bunch of Asians. Contrary to the other early retirees, he has taken an interest in the Chinese students. Yesterday afternoon when I was about to take them for a ride to Vejen Art Museum he suddenly showed up and wanted to join us. I couldn't see any reason why he shouldn't. There was enough room in the transport-vehicle which is equipped with extra seats.

When we drove under the bridge by the station and into Vejen itself there were quite a few people out shopping. Whereupon Malte began waving. And boy did he wave a lot. He sat there in all seriousness and moved his hand back and forth at everyone we passed. And it wasn't long before the Chinese students caught on. There were, of course, many of the shoppers who, slightly confused and out of sheer politeness, waved back. And I got extremely annoyed because it made it look as though we were a bunch of crazies out on an excursion in our institution's minivan. It wasn't exactly the red carpet treatment that Knud would get when he returned home from one of his expeditions. He was treated like a hero no matter where he went. Even in the US people would stand in throngs waving and shouting as he came riding in his open car. As had he been an astronaut or president. Yesterday afternoon it was just me and Malte and the Chinese students.

I Receive a Text Message from Amina Two Hours Later

as I make my way down the tower staircase with my mind full of pictures from Greenland. Among others, one in which Knud is standing looking across a snow desert as had he been a satisfied home-owner looking at his newly mowed lawn.

Amina is disappointed that I won't be coming. I had really been looking forward to it, she writes. She concludes with a sad smiley in which a tear is running down one of its cheeks and a broken pink heart.

A pink heart. What the hell has gotten into her?

Well, it isn't that hard to figure out. Amina has, of course, convinced herself that I've become so infatuated with her that I can't get her out of my mind.

And you really can't blame her, can you? She knows nothing about the money in the backpack, all she knows is that I have been contacting her more or less constantly ever since we ran into each other by sheer random.

But that's crazy, how can she actually believe that?

Well, let it be crazy, then, because it'd probably be a good idea to play along with it.

I hesitate for a moment, then I send her a pink heart back. Sometimes you gotta do what you gotta do.

A Whole Stream of Hearts Have Been Sent Back to Me in the Course of the Night

I discover the next morning as though Amina had been sitting up all night just waiting for me to respond, but that's how it is, isn't it, when you're in love? It's a kind of madness that you can't control. On the other hand, I'd like to know what Tom would say if he knew what was going on because the good-natured bear had a tendency to be the jealous type already back when we were young. And that sort of thing usually doesn't improve with age.

It's past eight and there will be a briefing over at the office for the teachers at eight-thirty right before morning assembly and god help the one who is late for Harris' meetings.

So I jump out of bed, but realize it might be a good idea to send a message to Amina which I do standing in front of the morning bread and touching the breakfast rolls that they bake right here, which is probably the best thing about the folk high school. And I mention it because when I look up her profile on Facebook I notice that she has put up photos of cakes which she has baked herself and that she follows the Great Baking Contest.

Welcome to the Day's Morning Assembly,

I say, come closer, find a chair sit down. Yes. Good.

Harris is sitting at the piano and commences to play the prelude to 252 and while "Through the snow herbs and bushes protrude" rises from the old voices, I patiently wait here behind the lectern for it to be my turn.

I can sense that my adrenaline is high because I wasn't supposed to be the one standing here this morning. The only reason why I stepped in is because the teacher who was supposed to conduct this morning's assembly had accidentally slipped on the icy road early this morning and landed in a ditch. I'll take it, I said when all the teachers were gathered for the morning briefing in the office. That's no problem.

I'll take it! I had said, because this was my chance to assert myself and show that I am a team player.

*

I actually think I make a great start, I begin by introducing the great hunter, Aqqaluk, who one afternoon is walking around Nuuk looking at the goods that have arrived on a big ship from Denmark with bananas and other things.

"That's how it was back then. When a boat arrives, well, it was just a matter of getting down to the harbor to see it because not much else happened back then. Remember, there was no internet or TV.

So it was very exciting down at the harbor, but here comes the point of the story. Suddenly, Aqqaluk discovers that there is a container that hasn't been lowered down to the quay berth to the other containers. It is simply left onboard the ship.

What's that? Aqqaluk wonders and goes to see the captain to ask him. And when the captain answers in a roundabout way, our hero becomes seriously interested in knowing more.

That same evening, after the drunken Danish captain has gone out like a light on the bridge, the hunter sneaks onboard the ship. As mentioned before, the container is the only thing standing on the deck.

Perhaps I should just add here that Greenlanders are deft with their hands, we are talking about an explicit tool culture so it was no problem for Aqqaluk to open the lock and unbolt the door.

He slowly opens the door, which is heavy even for him.

So far I can tell that I have all the old pensioners in the palm of my hand with my story. They are rocking their feet back and forth with anticipation and their eyes are wide open. No one is dozing off as is usually otherwise the case. The Chinese students haven't shown up, but I hadn't really expected them to. They are probably crossing the courtyard on their way to the classroom for the day's lesson, and I'm on my way there, too, but right at this very moment a Greenlander is standing on a ship.

Okay, where did we leave off? I ask. At first our hero can't really see anything, but then suddenly he can hear something bustling about in there and there is a permeating, rotten smell. Like old horse meat.

It's probably an animal that's still alive, he thinks. A bear, or something that will be going to Denmark.

Hello! he shouts.

There is no response.

On the other hand, some of the old pensioners give a start because I'm really engaged in this.

Hello! he tries once again.

There is still no response.

Okay, well, he didn't want to risk entering the container, so instead he turns the projector on the wheel house so all of its light, which is several 100 watts, is focused directly into the container. He gets a shock because he knows perfectly well what it is hovering in there. It is death. Yes, death itself is lifting its head and reveals a face that expresses more surprise than outright fear, he practically just waves our hunter away with a movement of his big, dirty hand.

And it may be that Aqqaluk gets afraid --- indeed, it is a matter of escaping before Death gets his claws into him, because once the genie is out of the bottle, so to speak, it's hard to put it back in again, so he practically stumbles down the gangway, almost falling as he does so, gets into his dog sled which he had apparently parked close by. He whips his dogs, quickly disappears, only to become a mere dot on the horizon that grows smaller and smaller.

Aqqaluk really believes it, he'll manage it because no one is faster than him once he gets his sleigh up to speed, well, no one, that is, except Knud. He'll be able to reach Thule already in a few days where he has some family he had planned to visit anyway for a little while. I can tell that my story is making an impression on them, the old ones, the thing about death which perhaps isn't so strange since it's something they can all relate to because they're all going to die soon, no matter how you slice it, they only have a small portion of their lives left.

With that in mind I think they have gotten just as much morning assembly as they can digest for one day so I wrap it up by saying that I'll save the rest of the story for Saturday on our way home from Germany.

And I can promise you all, you'll get Knud Rasmussen for all he's worth. There aren't many men of his kind today, let me tell you, but this was just a mere appetizer so you have something to look forward to on Saturday when we return from Germany.

I am standing Outside to Collect Myself a Little

before going to this morning's class.

The morning assembly could have been tackled a little differently, but it went tolerably well.

Oh. Harris' husband from Newcastle is out for a jog, I notice, as I start making my way toward the library. He is stretching by the handball goal, doing squats, almost as though he wants me to see it. He is wearing earmuffs and gloves. A few days ago he asked me if I wanted to join him. I said I would think about it. It seems he might be a little bored and is looking for a playmate, I've sometimes thought about what it is he actually does for a living. I think he may be a translator or something along those lines. Because he's a little pale looking.

We Are Now Friends,

Milovan and I, I notice when I, after a long day at the folk high school, am about to take a brisk walk in the light rain after supper. He actually responded with a "Yes."

I had actually planned to continue across the fields because it would probably have done me some good to get away from it all but I stop at the waterworks and start clicking around on my telephone because I now have access to Milovan's information which isn't exactly uninteresting to snoop in.

He is single, which must mean that he and the aunt got divorced. Gordana, yes, that was the aunt's name, I suddenly remember. They lived close to Ebeltoft. They didn't have any children themselves, as far as I remember, and it doesn't seem that they got any since then.

On many of his pictures Milovan is attending soccer games abroad, and I'm pretty sure it's the Serbian flag he has tied around his neck. It looks very dramatic, with Roman candles, banners and a lot of pushing and shoving on the platform.

Well, at least he's stopped that nonsense of trying to pass them off as Italians. It suits him much better not to. It really does.

Oh, and look! There's also a photo album of young, scantily dressed women which the amateur-photographer has taken himself. The girls are on their way to a lake, are standing in an abandoned workshop or lying in their bikinis on a beach at sunset. The pictures are nothing special, smooth in that fitted way typical for auto-mechanic shops but the models were surprisingly beautiful and long-legged. How did he manage to get ahold of them?

And there's more. In two of the pictures, Milovan appears in a blue uniform, that is to say, in his marine-blue pullover with black details and dark blue gabardine pants.

A customs official. Milovan has become a customs official. And in Billund at that, which is very close by.

Well, close by might be exaggerating it a bit, but Billund is only 40 km from Rødding, and what are 40 km today?

*

It's raining more now so I start walking back toward the the folk high school. It didn't turn out to be that long a walk, nevertheless, I have quite an appetite now and we're having Chili con Carne, one of my favorite dishes.

The cars that whiz past me on the main road drive through the water puddles, making the speedometer that has been placed by the road sign to light up with red numbers.

It's doubtful that Milovan can remember me, but who knows? He can see that Amina is a mutual friend of ours and perhaps he is able to put two and two together.

Or maybe he's just the type who accepts anyone who requests to be friends with him om Facebook. In order to get as many friends as possible.

I think Morten is that type because as far as I can tell the people on his friends' list can't all possibly be from athletic clubs and Novo Nordisk. There must be some false profiles that have slipped through, but who gives a screw about Morten because for a good while now whenever I've thought about Milovan I've envisioned that he was sorting oranges in Føtex. And all the while I have envisioned that he has in reality been working at Billund airport trying to catch airline passengers who aren't clean.

It annoys me in a way because I can't really let go of the orange images and it annoys me even more that he apparently still has quite a bit of contact with

Amina because I can see how they constantly like and comment each others' updates and pictures like there is no tomorrow.

When I Step Into the Main Building

where the portrait of the school's founder, Christian Flor, is hanging so you can sort of greet him every time you walk past him, I have a strange, rumbling sensation inside. It is a real messy incestuous affair that's been taking place, where the same blood between uncle and niece is mixed undiluted.

It wasn't even like that in Greenland, where they had their lamp game. I mean, there must have been *some* rules. Imagine if kids had resulted from it? They would have been pretty weird.

I only nod in passing at the group of early pensioners who are sitting with an open fireplace enjoying a glass of red wine or an after dinner cup of coffee. There are a whole bunch of empty bottles on the table and Birger-Bo is sitting slumped over half asleep.

Elvira casts a glance at me as though I really shouldn't be witnessing this. I don't care, because I've noticed that Birger-Bo tends to drink one too many. He drinks red wine with his dinner most days, because we have to remember to be good to ourselves, don't we? Followed by a nice little nightcap and then, for the sake of one's digestion, a little one the following morning.

Yes, throughout my childhood I learned all the signals and I can always immediately spot an alcoholic when I see one. Nothing can surprise me. She should only know.

I smile at Elvira and she smiles back.

Remember our excursion tomorrow, I say, giving a friendly grin as I continue up the stairs to my room.

I Turn Off the Light and Crawl Down Under My Duvet

and it is while I am lying in pitch darkness that all these old images of Amina start to emerge. I can now see what I was unable to decipher back then and that is that there was always a certain mood about her whenever her uncle was close by. A kind of naughtiness that shouldn't have been there. I just didn't notice it back then. Or didn't want to. How he was always sneaking around with his old camera and it was Amina that was in his lens.

The game I have only entertained in my fantasy has started to take shape in reality, the thought of which leaves me practically breathless. So he was running around there all along pretending to be the kind uncle who occasionally straightened a bikini top if it wasn't keeping the breasts properly in place.

And wasn't there also a time when Amina called and said that she would be delayed because she had promised Milovan and her father that she would be the "ball boy" while they played tennis in the brown pavilions? Yes, there was. So while she was running around in a mini skirt to run after little yellow balls, and whatever else she agreed to, I was hanging out in Frederiksværk under the assumption that everything was just fine. And when she finally did arrive she rambled cheerfully on as we exchanged small endearing embraces and youthful kisses. She told me that her father, that stupid deaf and blind oaf of a man, had had a bad back and couldn't play, so instead it had turned into a training session between her and her uncle. They might as well use the tennis court for something now that they had reserved it and Uncle Milovan and Aunt Gordana had taken the ferry over and all.

But what was it about her that made her do those things? Seeking out the light bulb like a nocturnal moth? We'll probably never know, because we can't always get to the bottom of why we do the things we do.

A mouse may be unfortunate and be born containing certain parasites that causes it not to run in the opposite direction if it smells that a cat is nearby, it may even, on the contrary, become hyperactive and a little curious. At any rate, it can't control itself at all and ends up getting devoured. When whatever is left of it comes out of the other end of the cat there are still living microbes in the excrement which a new mouse may sniff at and taste and the whole thing starts all over again, the cycle, because the house mouse has no idea what it is doing.

And I think the same goes for us humans. We have no idea what forces control us, what makes us attracted to deep water and I'd kind of like to know just how deep the water to which Amina was attracted to really was.

I Wake Up With a Jolt

The ferry and the hickey. I mean, that's totally crazy. It's not until tonight, after many year's delay, that the answer to that riddle has finally dawned on me: Milovan is the answer .

Isn't that how it always is? Several doors have to be opened before you finally get to the last one that slowly sucks all the life out of life in a way that is utterly mortal and immaterial because of course it wasn't the follower in Amina that got her to take that job on the ferry, which I have always thought.

And of course I had been focusing on the wrong things because it was neither the chef apprentice nor the mechanic who had like some sucking fish sucked on her neck but Uncle Milovan who had moved to Ebeltoft a little while prior to then.

I can only guess how it happened, how she every so often got off in Grenå so that they could do what they had to do. I can just see it before me. He would probably take her to various bathrooms in the ferry terminal. Perhaps he had his camper parked nearby or maybe they did it in the car, who knows?

I can't breathe properly in this darkness.

I feel like I'm being stifled.

I Step Out of the Shower,

rush over to my towel that is lying on the plastic chair in the corner of the cubicle I now find myself in. As a teacher I have actually been given access to a room with a toilet and bath but there is something wrong with my shower, I told the janitor once again this morning, but nothing is really done about it. When I turn on the faucet of the shower, so much water seeps out from the gasket that there isn't enough pressure by the time it reaches the head of the shower.

I'm freezing because the water was ice cold since they are apparently also stingy with their hot water supply here. And then there is some idiotic previous morning bather who has left the window ajar. It may be that there are stains of dampness on the linoleum floor and ceiling where paint is generally peeling off but those stains won't go away just because you open the window.

I slept like hell last night and that may also be why I'm freezing. All that stuff about Amina is still affecting me. What would Tom say if he knew what had been going on? That Amina had apparently been making herself available to her Serbian uncle?

And Milovan is a good friend of the family's these days, comes over on family visits, sits down at the dining table on Rønnebærvej. Perhaps he gives Tom a friendly pat on the shoulder and says there is just something he would like to show Amina in the camper he's always dragging around with him. Tom is probably clueless as to what's going on, but if he took the time to look out the window he might notice the camper rocking back and forth in the driveway.

No, I need to put these thoughts aside because they are draining me of all my strength and energy and they aren't really useful to me in any way. I'm going to have to focus on the upcoming trip to Germany, I need to concentrate on my big lecture.

The Folk High School Towel Is Hard and Stiff,

I could use a little fabric softener, but such is life at a folk high school. I'm not sure if this is really me, but let's see. Tomorrow I will only have been here for six days.

No matter what, I'm going to have to give it a chance or there'll be trouble. I am perfectly aware of that. I'm not that stupid. I can already hear my consultant at the Danish Association of Masters and PhDs with a frown, say "Oh, so that wasn't your cup of tea, either, I presume?" while stressing "either." "You do recall how things turned out at Living Institute?" That's easy for him to say and furthermore he more or less doesn't give a damn because the only role he has is making sure that he is occupied with something.

I could also just have chosen the easy path and studied to become a lawyer like Lone, then I would have been sitting pretty, but it's also a matter of holding on to your dreams, because that's what makes us whole and living human beings.

My dreams, I reformulate to myself, because they were the ones Lone terminated when she stepped into my life. Literally stepped into my life because when she went to a concert with her study group to get a break from their many exams, I was the one who stood on stage with my band. And we played our own material, in fact, not a bunch of cheap cover songs that Birger-Bo listens to with his windows open. 'Cause I've discovered that he's the one (who else?) that has a soft spot for schmaltzy pop music.

But enough about that. After we moved in together, Lone and me, she wasn't too thrilled with my Thursday night rehearsal sessions so I started going to them less and less. Finally the drummer and bass player, which was Asger, got picked up by some other bands because there is always someone who needs a drummer or a bass player. As for me, a stopper was put to my career in music, but I have later learned that Asger went on to become a stand-in bass player for the Danish band, Magtens Korridor, and he's even taken part in some of their studio recordings. I don't necessarily think that he has the proper talent for it, but he rehearsed an awful lot which can get you far these days, so never mind that.

The Door to the Hallway Opens.

I stand completely still for a moment. Someone slips into the cubicle next to mine and the lock is turned. No, you never get the chance to be alone just for one moment at this crappy folk high school and speaking of crap, I can tell you the individual next door has a whole lot that he needs to get rid of.

I discover that I forgot to take clean underwear with me from my room and since I'd prefer not to have to run up to my room to get a new pair I hop into my pants naked. The bus is leaving in about a half hour.

My god, the stench seeping in from the cubicle next door isn't for weak stomachs. In fact, it's unbearable, especially now where I'm standing here all clean and newly showered. For some reason I think it is Malte who is sitting in there, but I'm not sure.

But isn't that how the demented become? They degenerate and in certain ways become children again and can't control their bodily functions. Many of the elderly spill their food and burp when we eat dinner.

The Garden Gnomes in the Rear Window

So, you don't have the money,

is that what you're saying?

Yes, that's what I'm saying, I answer while crawling down from the bus again and looking toward the main entrance. Where are they? We were supposed to leave at 9 am, but it's 9:30 now and none of the pensioners have shown up, not a single one.

Where is the money now, then? my sister asks.

It's a long story. I'll tell you later, it isn't a good time right now. I've got a lot on my mind at the moment, if you must know.

What is it?

I really don't feel like talking about it, I answer.

Okay, Birgit responds, fortunately she instinctively knows not to ask me to elaborate.

That's the kind of relationship I have with my sister. She is actually two years older than me but I've always been mistaken for her older brother. When she became a medic in the defense force I went all the way and got a university degree. I'm also more than 30 cm taller than her. That might also be why.

At any rate, she's incensed at the moment which I can understand because back home in Frederiksværk my mother has apparently gone on the wagon and she's been serious about getting those carpenters started—

indeed, from what I understand the entire apartment is full of carpenters and while they are busy working at the house she is running around in the forest in Frederiksværk. For she has gotten completely obsessed with exercise. I guess you could say it isn't so strange because when the lid has been put back on the bottle it's got to be replaced with something that has just as much punch as the liquor. It's got to be something that really works and can take over your life. It could be Jesus, it cold be sex and it could also be hard exercise which releases all these wonderful endorphins in your brain which you quickly get dependent on. Because it's the endorphins that make you run even if you don't feel like it and the weather isn't suitable for it. But you can't resist it because it makes you high. The endorphins ensure that. The endorphins are your friends.

*

Okay, I'm going to have to go now, I say to my sister when the driver starts the engine and I see some of the pensioners finally emerge from the courtyard as they start to make their way in a long, wavering line toward the bus.

I myself get onboard. The Chinese students are

already sitting down in a silent cluster on the seats furthest back. I'm starting to think that it is becoming increasingly strange that they are here because even though there are some half-hearted attempts to include them in activities, as for example, this trip to Flensborg, nobody really knows what to actually do with them. They seem so lethargic. But that's perhaps not so surprising, because they don't get much out of the morning assemblies or from singing from the folk high school song book. And what do they really need with the Danish lesson, when it comes down to it? Why haven't they gone to England to learn English instead? Or to Spain to learn Spanish? At least you can use those languages in the world, but Danish? To be honest, and I don't see why we shouldn't be, I'm afraid we're in a real money-making operation. Each student causes a certain amount of money to be issued by the Danish government. In other words, we're taking advantage of them. Yes, that's precisely what we're doing, giving them stupid Danish names and moving them around to different places so we can get our funding.

And they put up with it. They put up with everything. Perhaps that is the only way, I'm thinking as I sit down on a seat in the middle of the bus, a society with a population of over a billion, or however many there are, can function properly. You have no choice but to adapt.

Something which, the early pensioners, who are now crowding into the bus, wouldn't dream of. They question just about everything. This morning they were angry over the fact that they had to prepare their own lunch sandwiches for the trip. They have paid such and such an amount for the course so there really should be enough money to eat out somewhere, they claimed. But it didn't work. Maybe that's why they were delayed.

They sit scattered about in the front of the bus, because that's what they've been used to their whole lives, sitting up front. Harris, who gets in as the last one, takes her seat which is, very naturally, next to the driver. Which means that I myself am sitting in a rather deserted part of the bus. Which is perfectly fine. Knud didn't fit in anywhere either because he was neither a Dane nor a Greenlander. Knud had to create himself, just like I do. There's no way around it.

It's Simply Not Good Enough,

Harris says to me when she, shortly after we cross the German border, sits down next to me.

At first I'm not entirely clear on what it is she's referring to because I didn't get much sleep last night so I was dozing off a bit, but I am quickly able to surmise that it is Agertoft Trafik she is mad at. It is the bus company that is driving us today and the one the school normally uses.

It ought to be evident to them by now that we need the big bus which include toilets.

Yes, you've got a point there, I say.

Up until now we've been forced to stop at two rest stops so they could get off and relieve themselves. From what I understand it's the same at the folk high school, where the old ones are forced to run out and pee every so often in the middle of the lectures.

Harris and I chit-chat for a little while the way you do when you're sitting in a bus, and I sense that she relaxes in my company. In general we get along pretty well together but I also believe that the successful morning assembly I conducted yesterday has contributed to that fact. She's begun to realize what I stand for, I think, but wait 'til it's my turn again on Saturday, because that's when I intend to go all in.

She had actually planned to remain living in England, she tells me, but she needed the extra money.

Well, money never hurts, I say, thinking of the money in the backpack up in Hundested and which is so utterly out of reach at this point that it is actually troubling.

*

Something or other is taking place up front. There is a staticky sound coming from the loudspeakers. It is Birger-Bo who has sat down in the seat next to the driver now that's it's vacant. And he has, by god, gotten a hold of the microphone.

Dear friends, he begins, since no one else has taken it upon themselves to introduce our Chinese co-travelers to the history of southern Jutland, then he will be happy to do the honors.

And boy does he give them the full history, right from when Dannevirke was created in the Iron Age to when the Prussians defeated us in 1864 and right up to when Christian X rode across the Danish-German border on his white horse in connection with the Reunification in 1920.

But of course none of this seems to make any

impression on the Chinese, I can see that they can't follow it at all, and I understand because the flat landscape we're driving through is nothing but that, flat, and Dannevirke couldn't possibly make any impression on anyone who has walked on the Chinese Wall. Come on! And as far as the Gold Horns go, which Birger-Bo is giving a long and thorough description of, well they are nothing compared to the terracotta soldiers which were discovered in Xiang in 1974.

There was a program during the fall on Danish TV about those clay soldiers and it's gotta be the wildest story I've heard yet.

As far as I remember it, a local farmer was digging a well for himself, when he came across an amazing clay head. Now that was what you call workmanship. With fine chasings, choice molding, the works. And the archaeologists that came to see it were also extremely excited about it. Then one of them said to the other one that perhaps they should continue digging a little to see if there was more, maybe even another clay head. And boy did the ball start rolling from then on. Not only did they find other clay heads, but entire clay soldiers, one after the other, and it wasn't long before they also discovered clay horses and clay chariots and they were all life-size.

It was one gigantic underground army of soldiers: on horseback, standing and kneeling.

They started digging in 1974 and they are still digging. It's totally mad. So far they've found 8000 soldiers equipped with various forms of weaponry, 530 draught horses, and no less than 130 carriages.

So you can pack up your gold horns, Birger-Bo, yes, spare us your ridiculous little hooting horns.

I Throw My Small Piece of Luggage on the Bed

and walk back out to the carpeted hallway. We've agreed that we are free to do whatever we want until supper which will be at Gnomenkeller which is right next to the hotel. And right now it is a matter of getting out the door in a hurry so I won't have to accompany any of the others.

And yes, it is sheer bliss being able to stretch one's legs and strut all alone down the pedestrian street where there are plenty of specialty shops on both sides. I quickly notice that they have certain kinds of shops down here in Germany which the point of which I don't really understand. Take the one called Rossmann which has a selection that spans just about every genre: soda, umbrellas, creams, cookies, nail polish, herbal tea, two shelves filled with toothbrushes, chips and wine. In other words, it's neither a pharmacy, a kiosk, a supermarket nor a health store.

Yet still it seems that those who enter and leave the store, the customers, are fully aware of the kind of store they find themselves in. It is fascinating. This is the kind of shop that indicates that we humans have a need to hold onto and categorize things in our world to make us feel safe even though, when it comes down to it, everything is blurry and floating around. This might even be material suitable for another morning assembly lecture. Because I can imagine that if we just took a closer look we'd discover that many things in the world are like that. For example, in Bilka's Fruit and Vegetable department where all the citrus fruit: oranges, mandarins, blood oranges, and more are neatly packed in fruit boxes which Milovan back in the day merely had to carry out to the shop. No problem. But if we, as a part of a thought experiment, placed all the different types of citrus fruit that actually grow on trees around the world next to one another in a row the transitions between them would be so seamless that Milovan wouldn't have a chance in the world. He simply wouldn't be able to tell when one fruit starts and the other ends.

But I had better watch out now because I'm suddenly beginning to feel oddly drained and disheartened. It's as though something chemical is seeping out from my muscles and organs and is slowly poisoning me. I don't know where it's coming from and now I'm suddenly down at the pier and I have no sense of actually leaving the pedestrian street.

*

Two men are fishing at the quay. They have managed to catch quite a few fish which they have put in a pail. They are still moving and their scales are glittering in the pale light of the sun. It's really getting unbearable so I start making my way over to some stands that have been set up closely together not too far away. It seems it is a Christmas market in which hand-made wooden figure,s crocheted hats and warm slippers are sold. There are also some stands where they serve sausages and beer. If you have more of a sweet tooth there is a stand with roasted almonds and gingerbread.

One beer can't do any harm. It might even be a good idea, that way I can try to collect myself a little, because what is it really that's wrong with me? I don't usually feel this way. I am constantly oscillating between feeling powerful and weak, first powerful, then weak, and then powerful again. It's really not very good. I honestly don't really know what I can do about it. But don't ponder too much over what can happen, I say to myself, because there is so much that could happen.

Elvira

Isn't that Elvira? Yes, she is standing a little by herself next to a tall table. She is, of course, holding a cigarette in her hand. It's as though I'm looking right through her and seeing what's on the other side of her, all the way to the industrial harbor on the opposite side of the fjord where a crane is rummaging through some old iron.

I consider for a moment going over and talking to Elvira. I feel like doing it, but I don't really have the courage. While debating with myself on what to do I notice she's not alone because the man from Gram suddenly appears, he with the thick hair and the watery blue eyes. He is smiling from ear to ear and carrying a small gray mug of Glühwein in each hand. Look what I've got! She takes one of the mugs with just as big a smile and puts the cigarette in an ashtray.

What is she doing with the language teacher? I thought he was the one who was going to see to our Chinese students, show them the Danish-German cemetery, the Duborg School, go out of his way a little. Instead he's standing there turning on his charm. It's as clear as day. He is talking with his mouth, thick hair and hands while Elvira forgets all about her cigarette burning up in the ashtray, which normally takes a lot.

I think I know what's going on because he has a blissful look in his eyes. Right now Elvira is the focus of all his attention. She's probably been the nice girl all her life but right now, just before closing hour, she's gotten a need to let herself go a little. You can't really blame her and it serves Birger-Bo right because I can't forget the way he treated me on one of the first nights.

Somehow I managed to say in a rather clumsy way, without actually saying it directly, that I had recently gotten divorced, something which he was somehow able to make a big deal out of. Among other things, he claimed that it is only the weak who succumb to getting divorced instead of riding through the storm. I felt that he was trampling on me and one should never trample on those already lying down because let me tell you, you big conceited asshole, that what you said, Birger-Bo, not only nags me, it also hurts, and I'm going to make sure you don't get away with what you said without getting properly punished. Just you wait, you good-for nothing pensioner on early retirement!

It Is Almost 6 PM

and it is already dark outside when I arrive at Gnomenkeller. I have to walk down a few steps because the restaurant is situated one meter below street level. I walk through the room in which the ceiling is low, there is heavy brown furniture on both sides, hunting horns, and big mugs made of porcelain hanging on the walls.

I have to go down all the way to the opposite end because the pensioners have gathered at a short bar counter where draught beer is being served to those guests who are waiting for their table. And of course they are standing here because they never miss a thing, not a single thing.

I make the rounds, greeting them all, and order the beer I was cheated out of earlier. I attempt to order in German, which goes rather well because for some reason or other I chose to major in German in high school, but no matter, because I now see that Elvira has sat down next to Birger-Bo.

Everything seems to be absolutely fine, but it isn't because Birger-Bo is clearly intoxicated. Elvira is trying in a rather worried and ashamed way to cover it up by chit-chatting a lot, but he doesn't listen to a word she says, juts keeps drinking his beer with a listless expression on his face. My guess is that he paid a visit to that Rum factory he was talking about long before we left for Germany and that that's what's keeping him going.

A mood of unease is spreading among the pensioners because it smells a little of grease and fried potatoes which has probably made them hungry. I notice that three long tables have been reserved for the folk high school, something which has been arranged by Harris, of course. She knows how to do that sort of thing, always predicting what's waiting round the next corner. Also when it comes to the social aspect she's on top of things, talking with everyone as she spreads her cheerful mood. She has a certain talent for the folk high school life.

We start to take our seats at the table, there is the sound of screeching chairs, but not until we are all seated do we discover that Malte is not here and someone says that he probably went upstairs to lie down for a rest. From what I understand, his mind is really deteriorating.

But there are more people missing, we realize. The Chinese students, of course. All seven chairs are empty. Why they aren't here no one knows, but it's clearly not good, of course..

Harris, who is the only one who remains standing behind her chair, asks whether any of us have seen our Chinese friends during our walk around town earlier today.

Oddly, no one has. The center of town isn't all that big.

I look over at the man from Gram who is sitting turning his glass on the thick tablecloth, pretending as if he isn't following our conversation in the least bit.

Yeah, you're full of it, I'm thinking, because it had clearly been agreed on that you were going to be in charge of them, but you had been busy with a lot of other things instead, hadn't you?

Two waiters position themselves at our table with notepads, but we're not at all ready to order, we haven't even looked at the menu yet so after ordering a round of beer on the folk high school Harris sends them away.

*

When the food is carried out many of the old people, especially the men, hurl themselves at it as though they'll never get food again. I have ordered a schnitzel which looks very good, I can't say that it doesn't, but I suddenly don't like it. It's the thing about the Chinese students. I don't like the situation. They can't just vanish into thin air like that. I manage to cut a small piece of meat and put it in my mouth before making what is called a snap decision.

I get up and without saying anything to others I leave. The man from Gram looks at me stupidly.

I walk up the stairs to the street and enter the hotel which is right next door.

I greet the woman at the reception, continue to the first floor where our rooms are and I don't get far down the hallway before I start to hear the sound of low Chinese voices behind one of the doors. So this is where they are, they have gathered in one of the rooms. Have they just been sitting in there all afternoon? It's not just a little weird that they haven't considered going out to look at the new and strange city we've arrived at, what with all it has to offer.

Perhaps it's because they weren't properly informed about what the plans were, maybe they were waiting for the man from Gram.

I knock on the door. At first there is no response. Then a head pops out of the door and looks at me with an empty gaze, as though it is waiting for something.

I think this particular guy is Frank, but I'm not sure because I'm starting to find that they look very similar to one another, the Chinese students. How can that be when the terracotta soldiers back home in Xiang have been adorned with the finest and most exquisite details? And these are real paper of flesh and blood and not made of clay.

I ask him why they haven't come down to the restaurant.

He looks at me with an empty gaze, as though he doesn't understand what I'm saying.

Behind him the others are sitting spread out in the room, on the floor, on the bed, in the windowsill. And Malte is sitting there too. In a way it is strange and yet it makes sense because he is losing it a little and the group has probably picked him up and seen to him because that's how they do things in China.

We could learn a little from that.

In the Rear Window of the Bus Is a Garden Gnome

which one of the Chinese students has bought and which is staring out into the world, so they must have gone out and explored the town at some point. They followed behind me in single file on the way back to the restaurant and to our great surprise Grille Haxe and other German specialties turned out to be to their liking. I must admit I hadn't seen that coming.

According to the schedule we are supposed to depart in half an hour, but we'll see. I know that Harris has made it very clear that we must remember to visit the restrooms before leaving so that we don't encounter the same difficulties that we had on our way down here.

Bing, I hear the familiar sound from my telephone.

It is my mother. She writes a short message that she doesn't mind celebrating Christmas alone. I'll be perfectly fine, she writes. I've put up a few extra decorations and will cozy up with Sita. She's given the dog a bubble bath so the whole place smells of dog shampoo. She has sent a picture of the poor creature who is sitting all wet and utterly confused on the living room carpet, wrapped in an old towel.

But that wasn't part of the deal. We had agreed that

Birgit would celebrate Christmas with mother and look after her a little.

I try calling my sister but she doesn't answer the phone.

Of course she doesn't. I start composing a sharp message to her but she beats me to the punch. She has seen that I am trying to get a hold of her so she writes that due to a lot of illness, both among the permanent staff and the temps, she has been forced to take some extra shifts.

It is, of course, not something I would wish for because, as you can imagine, having to spend Christmas in Vordingborg Barracks isn't exactly a dream situation for me. But there is nothing I can do about it.

She's full of it. I know exactly what this is all about. She is trying to avoid mom. Now it's her turn to have a guilty conscience and she doesn't know how to get rid of it. And not only has she taken the money, she's also spent them because, from what I can surmise, she's already bought a trip to Florida, Miami. The date is set for sometime in February. So she wouldn't be able to pay the money back even if she wanted to.

But you can't really, either, can you? Since you don't have the money, right?

No, perhaps I don't have it now, but it's waiting for me in Hundested.

Or is it?

I'd Better Get Going,

the bus is soon ready, it's backed all the way up to the hotel and I am just about to grab hold of my suitcase when Rasmus calls on Facetime.

Hello, Rasmus.

Hi.

How's it going? I ask.

Good.

I can see that he is sitting in their designer kitchen with drawers that shut softly and without a sound, and there is no doubt that everything in that damn kitchen has the same perfect finish. On the other hand, it is all in black wood and steel and stone which was, from what I understand, in fashion last year. And that thing with a cooking island with an over-sized exhaust hood is so old school.

What are you up to? I ask.

He shrugs his shoulders. He could use a haircut. He's inherited my spike-hair that turns blond in the summer. He is a good-looking boy.

I can hear the others bustling about behind him, I can even make out their shadows and I see that they are setting the table for a big breakfast including juices, toasts, yogurt and a whole lot of Morten's healthy kernels and seeds. Lone is laughing at something in the background.

I'll be back home soon, I want to say, but that's not true, I won't be back until after New Year's. So say something, kid, I think. Why doesn't he say anything? After all, he's the one who called.

And it doesn't help that Morten, that tall, idiotic bastard is witnessing the fact that I don't really have anything to talk about with my son. While they probably normally yap away about athletics and stupid family programs.

I'm in Germany now, I begin. I'm sitting in a hotel room in Flensborg. The bus will soon head back to Rødding. It's been a very good trip. Maybe we should take trip down here together one day. Wouldn't that be fun?

Rasmus nods slowly.

Hi! I hear a voice say and Lone's face appears on the screen, She is wearing a light blue t-shirt.

How's it going? She asks.

On the whole pretty well. We're on a trip to Flensborg.

Yes, I just heard. Are you enjoying it? The job at the folk high school, I mean.

Although she had gone along with the fact that I

needed something to happen in my life after the divorce, she wasn't expecting me to do something so drastic as considering a move to Jutland.

Yes, it's very rewarding, there are lots of interesting lectures and I'm thinking about getting back into music. That's what you do at a folk high school, after all, isn't it? There is room to be creative here. We have access to a big music room so in that sense things couldn't be better.

We talk about how things are going overall and they are going well.

I sense that things have quieted down considerably around the breakfast table. Probably because Morten is listening in on the conversation even though he's pretending not to. But he is, of course, I would have, too.

You know what? Lone begins. While we were cozying up with some pre-Christmas activities yesterday we started talking about how it would be good for the boys, especially during these dark months, to get away a little, maybe go for a trip, you know?

That's true, traveling is good, and to travel is to live, isn't that what they say?

Yeah, so we ended up spontaneously buying a trip to Ketchup, Thailand, for the Easter break. But I didn't realize that that was actually your week, perhaps it was a bit hasty of me, but I just wanted to check and make sure it wouldn't interfere with your plans.

No, I can make it work, if that's what the boys want...

Rasmus nods very eagerly, gets up and leaves.

I realize that Lone was the one who got him to call me so that she could make this announcement. Which is so typical of her. How very tactical, you stupid bitch.

Nice t-shirt, I say.

Thanks!

But only if it's okay with you, she says as she brushes some hair away from her face.

It's fine with me.

It sounds like a very good idea, I add.

Well, enjoy the rest of your stay in Frankfurt, then.

Flensborg. I'm in Flensborg, I correct her.

Okay, fine. And have a great Christmas!

*

After we've hung up I feel completely drained and start walking around in my little, German hotel room because deep within my soul I realize what is happening. Lone is busy establishing a new family in which our two sons are incorporated, my two sons, and there is nothing I can really do about it because Morten has the ability to buy access to that which was once my role. I've also heard rumors that he's considering investing in a small speed boat. The boys would love it if he did, any idiot can see that, and so we can talk from now until doomsday about how love, compassion and biology are what truly count and that you can't buy love but that's just a load of crap because how much are those pair of mittens and the knife I bought at the Christmas market worth compared to trips to Thailand and a speed boat? I can't possibly keep up with that rat race. I don't stand a chance because such a hierarchical system is concealed behind everything we do. We just refuse to see it. When I was in ninth grade I bought a rat with my own money. Milou was its name and I was crazy about it, I would cuddle up with it, bathe it in a tub and teach it tricks, but it was mostly crazy about my father. As soon as he stepped into my room it would run around in circles with enthusiasm, actually as soon as it sensed his presence in my room. It took a long time before I discovered his little secret. He would always quickly suck on his finger before putting it into Milou's cage so that it would taste of toothpaste, cheese or whatever he had just had in his mouth –and, no, I'm going to have to go, we're about to depart because I can see the pensioners have started to make their way up into the bus. I watch them and discover that the rear window is now full of garden gnomes. They have been arranged in a row so they can look out the window all the way home.

The Chinese Cellar

The Trip to Flensborg Concludes with a Strange and Troubling Incident

which occurs just outside of Rødding.

Due to the doubt that arose in me in Flensborg, I wrote a friendly message to Amina, finely sprinkled with hearts just to keep the channels open and in response she sent me a skull.

An actual skull, no less.

Now what's that supposed to mean?

And aren't we soon home, so I can get out of this bus which is too damn slow because I need to get a hold of Amina, call her immediately, which I can't with all these people sitting around me.

Okay, finally, we have passed the city sign and the speed control which only indicates 43 km per hour and I see the big white buildings of the folk high school with the black roofs through the windshield.

When we swing into the final stretch, the gravel road flanked by old beech trees on each side, we pass a local bicyclist with a rather large Christmas tree strapped on the luggage carrier. He greets and smiles at us.

As I make my way up the middle aisle of the bus so I can be the first one to get out I hear the church bells clanging from the Free Church and I catch sight of a procession slowly walking behind a hearse as it rolls down toward the open double gate because it is, of course, a funeral and not a wedding, which I thought it was at first. A funeral where there are a lot of red roses scattered on the coffin, which is carrying a dead body, as though to emphasize the text message I received. Well, we'll leave that for now because the bus has now stopped so I jump down onto the gravel and practically sprint up to the main building.

I Am Walking in Circles Around Myself in My Small Room at the Folk High School

as the telephone with the skull is growing increasingly hot in my hand.

Why don't I just call her? I don't even know myself. But what should I say to her? How should I tackle this? What did her message mean?

For Christ's sake call her already! Tell her everything. Once and for all. After all, it is your money and you have a legitimate right to it. And aside from that, at this point it's just a matter of getting a hold of it, no matter the cost.

I press the green button and a staticky sound can be heard.

I hear a click.

Hello? Says a deep male voice.

Of Course, Tom Is the Worm in the Apple

because he certainly makes it clear what he thinks and there isn't much of a folk high school teacher about him, let me tell you. It is more reminiscent of an engine station, tractors and a bear-voice that sounds like it comes from deep within the dark forests and which must have gotten deeper over the years. He will not tolerate that I keep sending his wife hearts, the voice says.

I answer that that wasn't at all my intention or what I had planned to do, it's just that I have been so unfortunate as to forget my backpack containing my inheritance from my mother when I ran into Amina in Hillerød and that is why we are in contact with one another, yes, that is actually the only reason and that it is, in fact, it, the backpack, which is standing on the floor of their house in Hundetsted, that I want to get a hold of and nothing else.

Silence, for a very long time on both ends of the line.

And then I hear what sounds like a loud growling through the telephone line, making it clear to me that I can just forget all about that and if I ever so much as show my face in Hundested, well, then...

I Could Murder Tom,

simply murder him. What kind of a person is he? He was already an idiot back in high school, a heavy dumb-dumb, but that doesn't really solve my problem. It's also partly my own fault. I have been careless and stupid enough to postpone the whole thing, just waiting around without actually doing anything and now everything's just completely out of my control.

I need to take a different approach.

I Have Gone up to the Tower Room to Finish Preparing My Lecture,

I sort of have to because I assume that everyone's expectations are extremely high after my morning assembly, but it's as though I'm not really able to properly focus on it because my brain is racking itself to find a solution for my problems. Knud had his share of problems, too.

Okay, well, what have we got? When I was a child I thought the Eskimos were cannibals that would prepare the big pot and lick their chops when they invited guests from outside their community who would walk around the settlement looking at jewelry, sealskin boots and reindeer hide.

No, that won't do, it's much too personal and biased. I have also decided to drop the small detail about the Eskimos, together with the Indians, Bedouins and Africans, being exhibited almost a century ago in Tivoli and Copenhagen Zoo.

It's not that I don't find it interesting because I can just envision it, taking Rasmus and Casper on a Sunday outing to the Zoo, the sun is shining, we have passed the monkey caves and the elephants when suddenly we catch sight of some igloos and as we get closer we see men and women dressed in traditional Greenlandic outfits, there are also children and harpoons and sleigh dogs busy doing their day-to-day chores behind a barbed wire fence. It's kind of wild to think that that sort of thing has taken place here in little peaceful Denmark.

Hey, Tell me,

what are those Chinese students up to?

I'm pretty sure I can hear them running around in the hallways. A door is opened only to be slammed back shut. They are basically out of place here. They belong down in the cellar below the dining hall.

Their evening schedule has been canceled after the long trip to Germany and now they don't know what to do with themselves. I bet they look through the keyhole every now and then. In fact, that wouldn't surprise me at all.

Perhaps what's drawing them here is the fact that I am talking to myself out loud as I prepare for my big lecture tomorrow afternoon, reciting all that valuable information I managed to extract from the

research books.

Big dumb-dumb, Tom.

And Amina? It's probably been easy for him to convince her, that big follower, that this has something to do with stolen goods, tax money or something else and, apart from that, no one can prove that the money really belongs to me, so finders keepers, losers weepers, especially when dealing with such an exceptionally careless person like me who loses his money like that, etc., etc.

I'm at a loss as to what to do because I know perfectly well what that kind of money can do to a person. It can so easily ignite a certain kind of uncontrollable greed. Why did I even mention it in the first place?

*

I clear my throat, try using my voice again. Pull it up all the way from my stomach.

Knud himself was a powerhouse, a powerhouse, I'm telling you, and it is his kind of willpower that we need to put into words because Knud is a brother in spirit.

It doesn't necessarily mean having to break applicable rules and laws or going to the extreme in any way but every now and then it is necessary to consider what the situation requires and then just do it. We'll open a trading post and call it Thule and tomorrow we'll go on a quick trip across the ice sheet.

There are still little innocent sounds, subdued voices and quiet footsteps that can be heard coming from the hallway.

Enough is enough.

I get up and open the door with a quick pull.

No, there is no one. Are they playing hide and seek with me? Is that what they are doing?

I take a few steps out onto the brown stairwell, indeed, the steps and the railing are practically chocolate brown, and there are small pictures hanging there everywhere. Among others one in which some Dutch farmers are skating on a lake.

It's actually snowing. And quite a bit at that. Big white flakes are whirling down from the sky. A layer of snow is about to cover the domed skylight. It's probably still snowing.

I feel a small waft of cold air. I follow it, the coldness, and make my way down the stairs.

Now That I Have Come Down Here,

which is somewhere or other below the main building, there is no reason for me not to explore it, after all, Knud did it throughout his life.

After having passed a recreation room with a pool table from Søren Søgaard I must soon be approaching the Chinese students' kitchenette which has caused such a stir because I can already smell frying oil and some Asian spices: coriander, star aniseed and fennel.

They ought to show a little consideration, I've heard some of the early-pensioners say, however, I think that as long as they stay away from the main kitchen at night Harris has chosen to ignore their cooking habits because she is rock solid and avoids making things more complicated than they have to be.

And the Chinese students don't think the same way we do, which might also have been too much to ask. The Eskimos that Knud encountered didn't just jump into a pair of jeans or stop eating raw intestines from one day to the next, either.

Well, here it is, the little kitchenette and it's quite a pigsty, let me tell you. Old streams of sauce can be seen on the cabinets and a dishtowel is lying on the floor and I can see that dirty utensils have been put in the drawers. The two hotplates, which are really only designed for water kettles and ready-made soups, have old food stains on them.

There is something genuine and untameable about the Chinese just like there is about the Eskimos. They may not wear bear hide and they may not do drum dances either but like with the Inuits there is something authentic and real which cannot be dressed and confined at the Zoo because they don't seem to think so deeply about things. They are in tune with something outside of themselves just like the Eskimos were in Knud's time, but, unlike the Greenlanders, our modern, urban life is natural for the Chinese. As opposed to nature.

I have made my way past the kitchenette and have followed the hallway to where it breaks off and have now gotten so far down into the underground that I know where they are. From a door a little further ahead a stream of colored, synthetic light can be seen and this is where they are sitting in a long row, each bent over his or her own computer while wearing earplugs. They must be playing some sort of electronic shooting game because electronic shots and explosions can be heard.

Life is completely different than it was during Knud's time. I'll just have to accept that because that's what I have to work with.

They Sense I am Dangerous,

they must because they retreat every time I approach them. They hide, searching for good hiding places.

I have a firm grip on my weapon as I creep forward along the wall of the house, enter a house that has been bombed to pieces which is mostly an empty shell devoid of furniture or anything else. In a few places there are bullet holes that give you a clear view of the blue sky. I make my way up the concrete steps and onto the rooftop where the sun is beating down. It's very well designed, the whole thing, and the computer here at the office can apparently handle the graphics. It makes a rumbling sound every so often, but aside from that it works perfectly.

There they are! Nine to twelve of them are walking around in oblivion on a square that has a big tree in the middle of it that casts a shadow. They are standing in the middle of open space. Idiots! I load my gun, aim, slowly, slowly, taking plenty of time, pull the trigger.

BANG it says, accompanied by a whistling sound and the first one collapses down there which gives one such a satisfying rush that runs through the brain.

Confusion arises, they run in different directions but it doesn't help one bit because they have no idea where I am, so I knock them off, one by one.

There is also one hiding behind some oil barrels. How dumb can you be? Nothing good can possibly come out of that. I give the barrels a proper round, causing them to explode. Ha ha ha.

Now there's only one left, he's fleeing, thinks he can escape but he can forget all about it.

With an experienced hand, I jump across a low wall, jump down the three meters, land on the square and start chasing him. He runs into the tunnel which everyone has passed through at the start of the game. He thinks he's clever, but he isn't. Because it's a dead end with no escape route.

And now I've got him. His back is to the wall. All my Chinese enemies lie spread across the landscape.

I take a breath for a moment, cast a quick glance out the window, yes, they are sitting there on the opposite side of the courtyard, in a real panic and probably realizing that it'll soon be game over for them, Finito.

Back on the screen the last Chinese falls on his knees and lifts his head toward me. He is wearing sunglasses and a partisan scarf and extends his hands pleadingly toward me, but there is no mercy, these are the rules of the game, but just when I am about to empty my magazine on his chest I hear the sound of helicopters above me. Where the hell did they come from? The sky is covered with helicopters and the noise grows louder and louder, I know perfectly well what that means. They have brought in reinforcements. Of course they have. They've probably been transported all the way from China.

Now the first one lands and they all jump out, and there are a lot, let me tell you, and more and more are coming and each helicopter seems to contain hundreds of soldiers and they take their positions, standing, kneeling, lying down, and start firing like crazy at me but where the hell can I seek cover? It's quite an ambush they've managed to put together.

I resolutely get on my feet from the computer, run to the fuse box and turn off the main switch with a loud click and the next moment the entire folk high school is in complete darkness.

There. That'll teach them. Because all is fair in love and war and I wouldn't mind seeing how they are managing down in their black and dirty Chinese cellar.

One, Two, Three, This Is a Test

The Chinese Students Met Up

in a somewhat perplexed state this morning, and they never really got properly started on the vowels even though they have progressed quite a bit of late. I would actually even venture to say that they seemed a tad bit reserved without being impolite. Perhaps it really comes down to a question of respect. It was as though they were aware of the fact that I was the one behind their great defeat, that I was the one who had brought a curse down on them, that I had managed to accomplish that which only the Mongols and the Huns had done before me, namely, broken through the Great Wall.

I made a quick decision and assigned them group work to be done around the school so now I have the entire classroom to myself and am sitting here at the teacher's desk amidst the smell of chalk as I rack my brains and fiddle with my telephone. I press the round red button on the bottom of the display screen.

1,2,3, this is a test, I say out loud across the classroom.

1,2,3, this is a test, the gadget responds when I press play.

The lecture is pretty much finished, so that's not what's absorbing me right now.

No, what's absorbing me is Amina. I have gotten an idea. I want evidence, evidence that is strong and juicy. Something I can use against her if she doesn't cooperate. And Milovan is the one who will provide it. Tonight. He has indicated on Facebook that he will be attending an event at the Mascot. This is my chance. If I get what I want I'll be able to twist Amina's arm until her mouth opens and she starts coughing up my money because she didn't stop her little ferry trips, or whatever they were, after Tom came into the picture. And I wouldn't mind seeing that curly-head turn bright red in the face and aggressive if he finds out, so she better just give me back my money.

1,2,3 This is a test.

There. Everything's under control. Knud used to plan his expeditions down to the very last detail, too, he would lay out depots, check the weather forecast, feed his dogs. And even though I'm only going to Billund, it's not to be sneezed at, a mission is a mission and it's the details that count.

I check it just one more time. Right now there are six who have indicated they will be attending the Christmas lunch. Now there are seven. It's a a little sad, but what can one do in Billund when Lego and Lelandia are closed for the season? It is 6 pm, in other words, it's in two hours and there will be roast pork with the works, as it says on the menu. That doesn't sound so bad. I've always had a weak spot for roasted pork, but let's forget about the roasted pork for a moment, there is something else at stake here and Milovan is the end of the rope that I'll soon be pulling because I'm certain that once I start chatting with him over a beer and schnapps and roasted pork, he's bound to tell me something that I can use.

I feel like a completely new person. Something has changed within me.

It's Started to Drizzle

I notice up in my room while I am trying to decide what shirt to put on. I gravitate mostly toward the blue one, although that tends to get perspiration stains.

Hmmm, I'm not sure. Perhaps it would be best with a white or black shirt. It's worth considering. It shouldn't be left to chance. Once you are standing in front of your audience it's important to be properly prepared. At the same time I need to remind myself not to put too much into it. It's only a lecture. Sometimes they go well, other times not so well. And like I said before, I have other tasks lying ahead of me that are much more important.

I go out to the bathroom, drink some water straight from the tap, gurgle and spit it out in the sink. I look in the mirror. No, it'll be the blue one after all because it turns out I haven't taken any others with me. So we'll have to chance it. And why not? I feel well-prepared. I'll pull it off with power point and some charisma. I'll start off with Tom Christensen's poem which he wrote in connection with Knud's death, I know it almost by heart, but now I can hear the old pensioners bustling about in the hallway as they make their way to the lecture hall.

Yes, I'm on my way, my mind is clear, let's just get started and get the whole thing over with.

There Is So Much We Can Learn from Knud Today

I say and make a rhetorical pause as I look out across the audience.

For Knud was a powerhouse, a powerhouse, I continue. True, he may not have been all too tall, but nevertheless a great man resided within the little one, and he was the one who stepped forth when he arrived at the Arctics' settlement up at the end of the world where there was neither light nor heat. And Knud's enthusiasm was returned. There is no doubt about that. They received him warmly and offered him some of the intestines, particularly that of reindeer stomachs, that were so rich in vitamin-C which they couldn't get any other way. Because fruit and vegetables don't grow on Greenland. Neither back then nor now.

There. I nod to myself. I'm not going to cheat them out of anything, particularly not these small details that are so valuable, and I can see that it's really making an impression on them. There are no signs of the Chinese students anywhere, they are staying away from here.

I click on the next picture. Projected on the screen is an image of some men walking in front of some dog teams. They look rather exhausted.

If you're not in great shape or physically very strong,

having to live under the extreme weather conditions that Knud and his men had to endure as they moved about on the ice cap, dragging their sleighs and carrying their fully packed puks can be very tough.

I pause once more.

It wasn't just the cold weather that they had to contend with, if that's what you're thinking. It could also be things like altitude sickness, which could result in nausea and dizziness.

And then there was the issue of having to find their way in that landscape. Remember, there was no such thing as GPS or any other fancy devices back then. All they had to help them were a compass, the stars and imprecise topological maps. Knud knew how wrong things could go if they lost their way out there. There had been people who had tried it before them.

During the Denmark Expedition of 1907, Jørgen Brønlund and his sleigh team got lost in a deep fjord and completely they lost their bearings when they were on their way north to show that the northeastern part of Greenland wasn't an island but was connected to the mainland.

Six months later they found Jørgen Brønlund's corpse in a cave and on his chest lay his notebook in which he, with frozen fingers that could barely control the pencil he was writing with: Perished at 79', could no longer continue due to frost bite in the feet and the darkness. It is the reason why the other corpses are to be found in the middle of the fjord in front of Bræ (approximately 2 and half miles).

Many believe that this death note, which has been thoroughly analyzed and discussed for over a century, contains a hidden key, a mystery about a secret pact that it is rumored the men entered into and which some might say has been lost today, but let's leave at that for now.

We Are Sitting and Drinking A Little Red Wine Around the Small Tables in the Palm Walkway,

which runs between Flor's room and the entrance hall, and there are so many green and large-leafed plants that you almost get the feeling that they are reaching out for you.

It feels almost claustrophobic. I don't really go for palm trees and ferns.

My armpits are wet, but that's okay, because the lecture went well, I believe.

And why shouldn't it have? Of course, some of the oldies, like Birger-Bo here who is sitting next to me, thought perhaps that I was a bit too one-sided in my view of the role the Danes played on Greenland. But I can accept that.

Now Birger-Bo wants to know what it was Knud Rasmussen was able to do that was so great. He agrees that he managed much better than the Denmark Expedition which I may have emphasized a bit too much, but what if we were to abandon Greenland and focus on the people who have tried to battle with the cold in such such places as the South pole.

The South Pole?

Yes, and here I am specifically thinking of Amundsen

and Scott who really got their skis and sleighs going.

Well, I can tell you, I begin, that whereas Knud ventured out and encountered primitive man himself, that is, that which evolved right after the animals, the two gentlemen you mentioned were solely focused on planting a flag in the South Pole that had absolutely nothing to offer except their wimpy little flag.

I can see that I managed to shut his mouth once and for all with that one. He is sitting with his legs crossed as he rocks back and forth one of his feet.

Yeah, that gave you a little something to think about, didn't it Birger-Bo?

*

I pretend to be sipping my wine, but I'm not. It's a matter of keeping one's senses sharp and one's eyes on the prize.

My mother has sent a twinkling Christmas tree I notice when I discreetly check my telephone. A twinkling Christmas tree and nothing else. I wonder how she is doing. I suppose she's doing okay, my mother, she'll just need a little cheering up every now and then. I am looking forward to giving her the wooden salt and pepper set that I bought in Germany and when all this is over with I'll make sure to finally purchase those tickets to hear Denmark's Girl's Choir which she's so crazy about. I send her an angel and a Christmas star back.

*

We tried to save the folk high school as best we could, I hear Harris say.

She has been entertaining us with the story of how she and the previous staff managed to safeguard the crisis that hit all Danish folk high schools approximately ten years ago. I didn't follow it at all because back then I couldn't have cared less about the fate of the Danish folk high schools, but I recall talk of how they were no longer going to receive the funding they normally would get and which had kept them from going under for years. After they stopped getting funding many of them ended up having to turn the key for good.

Harris tells how they practically had to dig up students from the surrounding fields and pick them up in the lines at Netto Supermarket. Malte was one of them and he has been here ever since.

Harris can be funny when the situation calls for it. But on a more serious note, she tells how they at one point sold land upon which luxurious senior apartments were built. The idea was that the older people would come to the folk high school to eat their suppers and take part in some of the activities.

Okay, I'm thinking, that explains quite a bit because they are most likely the ones who make up a good part of the older students here. And I'm not entirely convinced that that's a good thing.

But gradually we managed to turn the tables, Harris concludes and takes a sip of wine.

This is probably where the Chinese students enter the picture.

Do you know when Greenland became emancipated from Denmark? Birger-Bo asks as he leans even closer toward me than he did before.

No, sorry, can't help you with that one.

Pause.

He looks straight at me and I look back.

It was in 1979. May 1st, he then says.

Okay.

Birger- Bo then asks whether I remember the little anecdote about death being discovered in the container which I never managed to finish.

Yes, I do. Since I was sort of the one who told it. I

had actually intended to finish it on the bus home from Flensborg but I didn't really get a chance to then.

If I recall correctly there was something about the container having to be flown in with a helicopter to the place on the ice cap where Aqqaluk was on his way to, it's actually a good story, but I don't feel like telling it to Birger-Bo.

Well, he says, there's just this detail that it couldn't have been horse meat that he smelled because there are basically no horses on Greenland.

You don't say?

Birger-Bo nods.

Jesus Christ! Will that idiot ever stop? I never asked for this, The man has no inhibitions and he is really rather boring company. And to be honest, I don't know if I can say for sure what the connection was with that container and death, I simply don't remember right now.

It's really seldom that I don't like people, but Birger Bo has managed to become an exception. He is really getting on my nerves.

Elvira gets up and leaves.

Are you going out to smoke again? I can tell Birger-Bo is thinking.

I put down my wine glass. I've hardly touched it.

It's time to leave. I'm not going out to smoke. I stopped smoking when I stopped playing music. And I'm not just going out to plant a flag, because like Knud I consider it my duty to penetrate things, deep inside, until I finally reach the spot where things start to become slightly painful.

The Conversation with Birger-Bo is Bothering Me a Little,

I must admit as I am crossing the lawn. I should have been more careful, should have foreseen I was about to talk my way into a trap. I really made a fool of myself there. But it doesn't matter now. I've got to move on.

I continue past the TV and newspaper room. Behind the Plexiglas window three older gentlemen are reading the newspaper and Malte is solving a Sudoku puzzle. Sudoku has become quite the thing among the elderly. It keeps the brain going they say.

The news is about to start on TV so they put everything aside.

I hear giggling at the place where the hallway turns a corner and I'm pretty sure I see Elvira with the language teacher.

There definitely seems to be something going on between those two, but you can't really blame her. I mean, it seems like Birger-Bo has really lost his marbles and, anyway, what is a marriage when you've reached their age and lived your entire lives together? What can possibly be left but the exchange of lousy moods during the day and foul smells at night? Many couples stay together until they can't stand one another anymore.

Lone and I didn't and that may have been wise. We knew when to stop in plenty of time.

*

By the time I turn the corner Elvira and the language teacher have already disappeared. They could, theoretically, have snuck into one of the rooms, I have no idea where their rooms are. Birger-Bo is probably sitting drinking red wine and rubbing his stomach over at the palm tree hall. Where have you been all this time? he'll probably ask when she returns at some point. What have you been doing all that time? You should know, Birger-Bo. Maybe it's none of my business, but does he really trust her?

I actually wouldn't mind if he once and for all found out what's going on because it would really punch the air out of his balloon, I imagine. He'd never get over it.

Elvira is a special woman and Birger-Bo doesn't deserve her. Neither does the language teacher, for that matter, even though he's started to wear ironed polo neck sweaters and in general making an effort to look better.

*

So now I'm here. I lock myself in my office. I don't turn on the light. The blue light streaming from the pause screens of three computers are more than enough. I open the small tin cabinet and take out the car keys to the folk high school's minivan because here on little Christmas Eve night no one will need it so I can borrow it for a few hours. No harm can possibly come of that.

THE BLACK CLOGS

As I Turn on to the Road Between Rødding and Langtved

the sky opens. It is suddenly pouring down in buckets, running down the car windows.

Damn! It's not supposed to rain on little Christmas Eve. It just isn't. As late as yesterday it looked as though it was going to be a white Christmas.

Since there is no other light than what the headlights are able to cut through in the darkness and rain, it's as though the tree silhouettes on both sides of the road are sort of arching above me.

I wonder if Milovan is even going to show up in this weather? Most people will probably choose to stay inside in front of the TV.

Indeed, there are even those who are forced to sit alone. My mother, for example. It's really inexcusable. And it's all Birgitte's fault. Promises should be kept. End of story. But you can never count on her, my sister. She's always done precisely what's expected of her, no more, no less. But your sister is your sister and always will be because blood remains thicker than water.

I suddenly realize just how far away I am from everything. And that there is very little I can do about things here. I miss everything back home. Not least my sons, Casper and Rasmus. I miss them so much it hurts. After all, it is little Christmas Eve. Even though they sometimes manage to get on my nerves. Especially Casper. He had a tendency to scream a lot when he was little. Fortunately, he's stopped doing that. But he's becoming a really bad loser and he's gotten the same hair cut as Morten. Anyway, right now it's a question of keeping one's spirit up, holding one's head up high and not letting your hand start to shake or display any sort of vulnerability whatsoever.

*

I turn on the radio in order to think about something else. And the voice of Jørgen Leth immediately penetrates through the little box to me, accompanied only by the sound of raindrops strumming on the roof of the car. It's still pouring down as hard as before.

It's actually really wonderful that Jørgen is keeping me company because the man usually has a lot on his mind that he is eager to share.

Tonight, on little Christmas Eve, Jørgen is telling about his life as a poet, film director and bicycle racing commentator.

He is almost on the verge of tears when he mentions

the hurricanes that on several occasions ravaged his home in Haiti, however, unsurprisingly, the topic quickly turns to that of the numerous women he's known through the years.

He confides to me that at an early age, and when he says early he means a lot earlier than the rest of us, he acquired the art of seduction and that throughout his life he has used that firm gaze of his, a gaze that contains genuine substance, to lure women into his bed.

I always thought it was the quality of his voice, which he, by the way, has started to sell as a ringing tone for telephones: "Answer the phone, it's Jørgen, answer the phone!" That did the trick, but if he insists that it's his gaze I'm sure he's right, but as I remember it, a guy like Tom would run around with a rather shifting gaze in his younger days as he kept a close eye on Amina, and isn't that in reality the same way you, Jørgen, used to run around in confusion around the finish line after the day's bicycle race as you in your atrocious French attempted to get an interview with one of the top participants?

So you know what, Jørgen? I think that in your old days you've become a little much and do you know what else I think? I think you are mostly seduced by yourself more than anyone because the truth is that you don't really have what it takes and, more importantly, you are no Knud, Jørgen. You aren't, even though you'd like to believe that you are. And you know what else, Jørgen? I'm going to press the "off" button. Hope you enjoy your own company, Jørgen.

I Look Both Ways

as I slowly roll down the main drag of Billund, because they've got one of those, in fact.

There. That's where it is. The Mascot. I park out back behind a big gravel area. I shut off the engine. Close my eyes for a moment and reopen them. Apparently the Mascot has an entrance both from the front and back and it resembles a western saloon a little, only there are modern billboards and and beer ads on the facades.

There is a good chance that Milovan is sitting in there completely oblivious to the fact that I'm on my way, but I am, I'm coming.

I take out my telephone. Place the knitted hat on it. Press the round, red button. 1,2,3, this is a test, I say out loud.

I listen. My voice goes through smoothly and clearly.

Now I'm ready. It's just a question of entering, retrieving what I came in for, and leaving again.

Milovan Looks at Me

as I carefully move the pixie hat lying on the table in front of me. My iPhone is lying underneath it.

I had assumed that Milovan was a bit of a loser who had to buy all his clothes at the supermarket. But that's not at all how he comes across in reality. He practically has a crew cut with high temples, he smells of men's cologne and he is wearing black Adidas jogging pants as well as a gold chain around his neck on top of a white t-shirt.

I can't say exactly what I had been expecting but it certainly wasn't this.

How old could he be now? Sixty-something? Maybe a little younger? It's hard to tell. His face is long and he has a narrow nose. He looks sinewy. Not tall and thin. Just sinewy.

What is it? Milovan asks.

Nothing I say and take a sip from my can of Royal beer which presumably must have been bought across the border and transported to Denmark from one of the border shops.

A part of me just wants to get up and leave, get away from this man before me, who gives me a feeling of uneasiness. I still can't put my finger on what it is precisely. But there is something or other, there's no doubt about that. Maybe it's his raw aura which I suddenly recall upon encountering it again. Already back then everything he did was taken as such a given that no one would ever dream of getting in his way.

And apparently that goes for today as well. The other regulars at the Mascot are meticulous about smiling and nodding at him acknowledgingly while at the same time keeping their distance. At least, that's my impression. He doesn't really belong in this bodega. With its fake decorative moldings and a pool table that is slightly too small.

My gaze catches sight of the skinny woman with tattoos on her bare arms standing behind the bar counter. She smiles at me.

I smile back.

She lifts a big glass of water as if to make a toast and I lift my beer.

She is wearing a worn leather jacket with tags and studs.

I decide that now is the right time to introduce the topic which is what I've come here to dig further into even though the atmosphere doesn't seem right for it. I just want it over with.

I saw your photographs on Facebook, I begin.

Of the many beautiful women, I say as I sneak my hand under the pixie cap and press a button.

The stewardesses, yes, he says as his thin lips glide into an unnoteworthy smile.

The stewardesses?

He tells me that he lives just outside of Billund and that for a period of time he rented his rooms out to stewardesses working for Norwegian and Air Baltic when they needed a place to stay between flights. He got some of them to permit him to take photos of them for a discount on their rent. He's always enjoyed taking pictures of naked bodies, he says.

Especially pussies smeared in coconut oil that makes them glisten in the right way.

I don't like the way he says "pussies."

I know that you also photographed Amina, I say.

Did she say that?

Yes.

He smiles once again in that dirty way.

I liked photographing her and she liked a little bit of this and that.

I understand that, I say, thinking of the gravel pit.

We sit for a while without saying anything.

You lived in Jutland, didn't you? I mean before you got divorced. You and Gordana.

Yes.

He empties his Ceres while he observes me.

We'll take one more, I say as I get up even though it's really his round.

Okay.

I hesitate for a moment.

Should I take the telephone with me or just leave it on the table? Neither one seems like a good idea.

I take it with me, holding it under the pixie hat even though it must look silly.

Hello, I say when I reach the bar.

The woman puts down a giant e-cigarette.

Two rum and colas. Double.

She gets to work on it. Finds two tall glasses and a lemon slice. She takes her time and is somewhat clumsy. Every so often she returns to the e-cigarette and takes a big drag.

I look down at Milovan who is sitting stiffly in his chair and staring out into space.

He is on the whole an extremely unpleasant person. but if I'm going to get anything out of it there's no escaping him. I take the two drinks the bartender has finally managed to make for me and go back to Milovan.

Milovan Does a Slight Movement with His Hips

before going out to the bathroom in an attempt to emphasize what took place in the cabins on the ferry because that was how it was: Milovan would climb aboard the boat whereupon he and Amina would sneak off to one of the little cabins where the staff could take a nap if they had had several shifts in a row. That was where the two of them would mess around on a much too small plank bed and exchanged hickeys because what had started out as photograph sessions developed into something else.

Rum and cola was what did the trick and my impression is that Milovan has told me everything there is to tell which in reality is quite a lot. He possessed a certain power over her which he retained also after she married Tom. She must have returned home to him and the kids with the kind of sweaty arm-pits you only find in the Balkans because she was caught in the trap, she couldn't refuse Milovan.

All of which I now have recorded om my phone, however, if Amina is a smart girl and gives me what rightfully belongs to me, everything will turn out fine.

I take out my iPhone from under the pixie cap.

Look toward the restrooms and press on play. Just to check.

Absolutely. Nothing. Happens. I can see the little dot moving across the line and on the display it says that there is a 28-minute recording but there must be something wrong with the sound because I don't hear any voices. What the hell? Did I forget to turn up the volume or what? Is that what happened? No, the volume is on full blast. What the hell is wrong? Have I fiddled too much with it? Was it all for nothing?

I'd watch out with that if I were you.

Huh?

It's the bartender. She's come down to my table. She is taller than I remember her, her leather skirt is pressing against the edge of the table. She is wearing numerous bracelets in different colors on those skinny arms of hers and she is holding the big e-cigarette in one of her hands.

I'm only saying it for your own sake.

Her voice is hoarse and her eyes look more concerned than anything.

I shrug my shoulders and say I just merely stopped by, that's all, and there was nothing...

If I were you I'd get out of here.

I was on my way, anyway ...

She keeps an eye on the bathroom door and tells me that if I wasn't already aware of it Milovan has on several occasions acted very unpleasantly toward some of her regulars.

She also mentions that he has participated in the battles for a United Serbia in Srebrenica.

She stares at me with her ocean blue eyes before saying the next sentence.

He is dangerous.

Yes, I was able to draw that conclusion myself, I feel like saying but I don't.

I get up, walk toward the door. I don't want to listen to her anymore. I've had enough. I want to go home.

One Moment Later I am Standing Outside on the Gravel Road Looking

at the Mini Van.

I reach into my pocket to make sure I have the car keys. I do. No problem there. I don't feel too intoxicated to drive even though I probably am.

Well, I really didn't get much out of this. Everything fell through. What went wrong? I am about to take out the telephone again when I hear a voice behind me.

Leaving without saying good-bye?

I turn around.

It is Milovan. He's put on a thin black coat on top of the white t-shirt.

No, but there's something with my mother, I had probably better just get going. Unfortunately, I don't have much choice.

In that case, the least you could do is drive me home.

His voice sounds very decisive.

You know, I ...

It's impossible to get a hold of any taxis tonight.

Then he says something in a very low voice which I can barely hear but which, against my will, forces me to step closer to him. It's as though he's pulling me toward him. That's the sort of thing he can do.

He repeats what he just said and this time I am able
to hear him.

I have something I want to show you.

What would that be?

Just drive me home and you'll see.

I look over at the WV.

Let's get going.

We Are Sitting at the Kitchen Table Eating Balkan Stew

which consists of a hotchpotch of meat and roasted peppers in various colors. I can't exactly say that it tastes all too great but I politely finish all the food on my plate as I wait to see what Milovan has up his sleeve. I honestly have no idea what it could it be and it is this

inert, stubborn strength of his that makes him so unpleasant. I don't like being here and his home also attests to a unique kind of individual who does things his very own way.

Worn down training machines take up the space of the entire living room to such an extent that you can hardly move around in there. It smells of goat.

Here in the kitchen it smells of fish. The door to the scullery is ajar and three dirty fishing poles have been placed in a row against the wall. He has told me that he has a lunch box in the fridge with sand worms. He has a gun safe in his bedroom that contains rifles.

Something is happening now.

Milovan pushes his chair back, gets up and looks at me for a long time.

Yes? I say, tired at this point from always having to be on the defensive.

Wait right there.

I nod.

He is only gone for a moment before returning with a big iPad. It is big and full of scratches.

He pours vodka into two glasses he is has put forth, all the way to the brim, reaches for his glass and makes a gesture with his hand indicating that I should do the same. Which I do. Yes, we might as well keep drinking now that we're at it anyway.

He presses on the screen and it lights up, he clicks on a file concealed in another file, presses on some other things and photos start to emerge, one after the other, positioning themselves as small squares all lined up on the screen.

They are all of Amina. She is posing more or less naked at various locations. The gravel pit was just one of many places, but I pretty much knew that. I both want to do this at the same time that I don't.

One photo in particular draws my attention. It is black and white. Amina is standing on a wooden floor with her legs spread wide apart and is lifting up the short skirt she is wearing, she is also wearing pair of white stockings and a ray of piss is streaming down from between her legs onto the wooden floor, creating a small pool under her.

The tennis pavilions. Of course. They were taken at

the tennis pavilions. The door behind her is ajar and there are some gravel courts in the background. She is trying to force a smile, but she can't seem to do it. Well, peeing at command probably isn't the easiest thing to do, either. I don't know when the photograph was taken but she has longer hair than what I remember her as having. She is probably somewhere between 18 and 20, with those banana-shaped breasts under her t-shirt.

I drink more vodka. The photos are rather small and I know that if I press on them they'll enlarge but I can't get myself to do that.

Milovan, on the other hand, seems to have no such scruples, as his, long, white, hairy index finger lands with a small sound on the screen and I don't know what to think now because a photograph unfolds in which Amina is sitting on the edge of a yellow chair and from her little narrow slit, which is encircled by light brown pubic hair, in what seems to be an added surprise, a thin candle is protruding. And, believe it or not, the candle is lit. And I see the white wax dripping from the candle as had it been a pipe that had been inserted inside of her and that it was her juices or his sperm that had been squirted in her and that is now being emptied out.

I Open My Eyes and Sit Up Abruptly.

Shut my eyes closed again for a moment. The headache I have is tremendous and it's terribly stuffy in here, there is a nasty stench of alcohol.

I lean back on the short wooden bed. I am in the same room that the stewardesses occupied when they rented it. We also looked at some of the pictures of the beautiful women who, with their colorful scarves and stiletto heels would come dragging their suitcases on wheels and take their lodgings with and be photographed by Milovan.

My clothes are lying neatly folded on a chair. My jacket is there, as well. I thought I had hung it up in the scullery. Perhaps I decided not to because of the fish smell. I don't know. I don't remember much because we ended up drinking more and more vodka. I must have finally gone out like a light. I can't get over how much power Milovan had over Amina.

I get out of bed and put on my clothes. Go out to the hallway. The door to Milovan's' bedroom is shut. He's apparently still sleeping. For a moment I consider knocking on the door but decide against it.

What time is it?

I take my phone out of my pocket. Almost 12. Christmas Eve's Day. I can see that Lone, Rasmus and my sister have tried to call me. I'm supposed to Skype with the boys later today so I don't really understand why Rasmus has tried to call. There is hardly any battery left. 12%.

Damn! I better get back home because in Rødding there will be a Christmas sermon at the church at 2 o'clock. It would be good if I could make that. And then there will be sherry served at Harris' house before the Christmas dinner. I've got to make that.

I go out to the kitchen. The light is still switched on, both in the ceiling and in the spotlights running below the kitchen cabinets. The radio is on very low. There is a cup on the table. The coffee machine in the corner is still on and there are still a couple of drops left at the bottom of the pot.

The black iPad is lying on the table at full display. I walk over to it and press on the screen. The picture of Amina's pussy with the candle. Something which I seem to keep returning to.

Suddenly a thought emerges that may have been below the surface all along but which is now unfolding in the back of my mind and which I immediately execute because what I do is take out my telephone and take a picture of the picture.

So far so good. Now it's just a question of getting out the door Perhaps I didn't get what I originally had come here for, but I got something else which may prove just as good.

I rush out to the scullery. Milovan could appear at any time.

My shoes. They aren't there.

I run into the bedroom in which I slept. They aren't there, either. They are my best shoes. Campers on the more expensive side which I bought while I was a project manager for a short while at Living Institute.

Try to think for a moment! You must have some idea where you placed your shoes. They can't just suddenly disappear.

Yeah, What?

I know I sound a little irritated because it's my sister who's calling while I am driving at somewhat too fast a speed wearing clogs that are slightly too big. I didn't manage to find my Campers, so what could I do? Finally I managed to jump into a pair of old clogs with heels and paint stains. Milovan definitely won't miss them. It was either them or a pair of rubber boots with dry mud stains.

But no matter. I haven't left Milovan's place empty-handed, and that's the most important thing.

Birgitte repeats that she can't get a hold of mother. I can clearly hear the concern in her voice. No, I'm sure you can't, I answer. And you probably should have thought of that before you agreed to take a lot of extra shifts. I also say a few more things without actually scolding her, and yet I feel it is about time to give her a piece of my mind.

Is she about to cry? Yes, apparently she is. But that's not really going to help the situation.

Despite the fact that I don't really feel like it, I start to console her.

I suggest that she get a hold of one of Mom's neighbors who could, perhaps, just check in on her. No harm can come of that and furthermore it would suit them just fine. Partaking in other people's misfortunes usually gives them a certain sense of satisfaction. I add.

Birgitte doesn't answer but continues to sob.

What do you think?

She still doesn't say anything.

Hello?

She's gone.

We've been disconnected. I automatically start to shake the tiny electronic device as though that might be able to resurrect it but it's no use. It's completely dead. The battery's run out.

I cast the phone aside and press down on the speeder.

I truly hope no one has discovered that the vehicle is gone, but why should they? There are no excursions planned until the days between Christmas and New Year's where the big buses will be used and not this van.

Maybe I'll even have time to put the car keys back where they belong and then quietly tip toe to the church and sing along to the Christmas carols.

*

I feel bad that Birgitte got so upset but she has only herself to blame.

But what about yourself? Are you really so much better than your sister when it comes down to it? What did you have to go to Southern Jutland for? She's your mother, too, or what?

Yes, maybe she is, but this time I wasn't the one who had promised to care of her.

I Notice

that the black car, a Ford, driving behind me, interchangeably moves way up close and then retreats back as though it's following me. It annoys me a bit because the road tends to wind a lot and there is considerable ongoing traffic. Lots of people who are on their way to different places to celebrate Christmas with their families. The cars are so filled with presents that they are actually piled in the rear windows and at least every other car has a tree fastened to the roof of it.

I put on the brakes a few times which seems to do the trick because now he's maintaining the proper distance. That'll teach him.

I don't quite understand why those clogs are too big for me because I'm considerably taller than Milovan. However, that's just how it is for some people: their fingers and arms and hands and other parts of the body might be bigger on them even though they themselves are smaller.

And, of course, even though I'd rather not admit it, I have given some thought as to the size of his member, what sort of a guy he stuck inside of Amina. Mine, for example, has an average size and I've never had a problem with condoms being too tight. But what about

Milovan? If he even bothered to struggle with condoms, that is.

*

There we have it again! The Ford. It emerges in my rear view mirror as route 132 has led me through numerous twists and turns of Føvling. There are two men in the car and it gets closer, accelerating on a long, straight stretch before passing me.

When it moves up right next to me and as the window is electronically lowered down, two short-haired men look in my direction. And then one of those infamous red signs with the word "Police" appears through the open window.

Something Wrong?

I ask the two police officers who have seated themselves in the backseat of my car. I can see them through the rear view mirror as my hands remain on the steering wheel. This may very well not be according to the book, on the other hand, it's started to rain again so I kind of understand them. But what is it they want? Where have you been? asks the officer who comes across as the older of the two and who seems to be the one who does the talking.

I've just been visiting some friends in Billund. We celebrated Christmas together which went fine and then I slept over.

Okay.

He nods with his big head.

I'm waiting for him to ask whether I've had anything to drink. I'd prefer not to have to blow into one of those alcoholometers even though it'd surprise me if I had anymore traces in my blood.

I say that I'm actually in quite a rush and that I teach at Rødding Folk High School and that there is, in fact, a Christmas mass scheduled there which I will need to attend.

I cast a glance at the telephone lying on the seat next to me which contains Milovan's pictures.

Is he the one who has sent them after me? Of course, you never know what effect local patriotism has on people, but, still, is that really possible?

Have I done anything wrong? I ask, trying not to sound desperate.

Yes, the younger one answers.

It's the first time that he opens his mouth. His voice is high-pitched.

I squeeze my grip on the steering wheel.

They said they saw me talking on the telephone without using the hands-free device already quite a distance south of Billund.

Oh?

That's illegal.

But, considering that it's Christmas only once a year ... the older one says.

Yes?

I don't know, should we let it go just this once? he asks, turning to his younger colleague.

Do we agree on that? He continues.

Yes. We'll let it go, the other says before I have a chance to say anything.

We just saved you 1500 DKK, the one sitting to the right says as they crawl rather sluggishly out each on their side of the car. It's as though the two officers have primarily had a dialogue between themselves which didn't include me but that's sort of okay as far as I'm concerned —as long as I escape getting fined and Milovan wasn't the one who sent them.

They tap on the roof of the car to indicate that it's okay for me to take off. Which I do. I take off like there's no tomorrow.

Elvira and Birger-Bo Disappear

I park the van

and tiptoe into the main building from the back. This is fine. I don't think anyone has noticed anything.

All I need to do now is put the keys back on their hook. For a moment the police officers really made me nervous but I've calmed back down. It's really a relief.

What time is it?

Okay, well, I can't make the Christmas mass. I might as well take a quick bath and then I'll be all ready and set for the Christmas dinner. It suddenly feels as though I have plenty of time. I'm not supposed to Skype with the boys until 3 pm.

I can see that the Chinese students have been at it again. They have placed some of the garden gnomes that they bought in Germany in various spots where they found room for them. In window sills, on dressers and other places. It's sort of cute. Perhaps that's the way they think we decorate for Christmas in Denmark. They are sweet, my Chinese students.

*

I unlock the door to the office when I hear someone approaching further down the hallway. I hurry inside and shut the door behind me. Voices. That are whispering. I'm apparently not the only one who isn't at the church.

All there's left now is putting the key back, but the little white metal cabinet is stuck.

Come on! Come on!

I pull extra hard and it pops open. I just manage to hang the car key on its hook and shut the cabinet door when the language teacher appears at the door.

We look at each other. I remain standing there in the middle of the room. I sense that there is someone standing there behind him out in the hallway, and you don't exactly have to be a genius to know who that someone is. I've also discovered something else: neither Elvira nor the language teacher have rooms in this hallway so I am pretty certain that their rendezvous take place in the new fitness area which has been set up next to the TV room. It used to be a music room but no longer is. In other words, I lied to Lone but it was a comparably small white lie, so it doesn't count. Anyway, it doesn't matter because I am certain that the Turkish bath and the Jacuzzi are very suitable places for them to do whatever it is they do together.

What are you doing? The language teacher asks, looking impatient.

Nothing.

What are you doing? I ask him in response.

He doesn't answer but looks at my much too large clogs before he ever so quietly disappears back out the door.

When He Disappears

I remain standing a little, take out my phone, the picture I took at Milovan's.

I press on the screen with my index finger and a number of options pop up at the bottom of the photo. I go into Messenger and send Amina the picture of the candle protruding from her vagina. Here you go. Just like that. A ticking time bomb is now in her inbox and when she opens it her world will explode. When the picture emerges on her screen she will grasp that I know everything about what was going on through the years.

And when she has gotten over the shock, she will tear her hair trying to figure out how I managed to discover her secret.

In a way I can't even answer that question myself because that actually hadn't been what I was looking for initially. It just happened because I more or less did what I had set out to do without really knowing where I was heading. In the same way that Knud never entirely knew what he would encounter when venturing off into the unknown.

I Know That the Boys Are Going to Call Me Very Soon

but when I pass the spa area I can't help stopping in my tracks. Are they still in there? And if they are what is the language teacher doing with Elvira? I just hope she can handle it because who knows what direction it might take, they both looked so flirtatious when they were standing by the booths in Germany.

I press me ear against the light wooden door that has a bit of an elongated and gnarled door handle, as though you were entering directly into a sauna.

I can't hear a thing. Not a single sound. Maybe it's all just something I've been imagining. Maybe they just stood chit-chatting a little before going each their own way. That is a possibility.

I am just about to leave when I hear a scratching sound, something like metal being dragged across the floor.

I carefully push the door and it opens, just a few centimeters, but that's all it takes for everything to come into my view.

Oh my god!

The language teacher is standing turned sideways and wearing a skimpy t-shirt while penetrating Elvira from behind as she leans across one of the three black dream beds that won't keep entirely still. They are totally into it, with her naked breasts swinging back and forth and everything, and I mean swinging seen from my vantage point. She's got her behind, which isn't exactly petite, posed high up in the air so he can properly enter her.

I'm surprised he's able to go through with it in that way because he's not exactly a young stud anymore.

I actually don't really want to watch this, it's really pretty disgusting, but the more you get the more you want, as they say, so I remian standing because I can't deny being somewhat fascinated and gripped by what's taking place.

Suddenly Elvira opens up her mouth and an ugly sound comes out of the delicate little woman as had she been one of the cows which I imagine were grazing in their yard back in the day. No, I'm afraid there isn't much sophisticated airs and fancy French wines over her right now, but rather barn animals and cattle grazing on the fields.

And Guess Who Comes Walking Toward Me

when I few moments later I walk out to the courtyard? Birger-Bo, of course, who else but Birger-Bo? On his way from the gym. The lighting isn't the best, which is probably why he has a flashlight swinging back and forth in his hand, but there's no mistaking that gait of his. He has pulled his pants all the way up and he has started to get those sideburns which many elderly men typically sport.

Hello Birger-Bo, I say.

Hello.

Have you seen Elvira? he asks with a perplexed look on his face which I can already discern before he reaches me.

Yes, of course he is out searching for Elvira because sooner or later he'll have to discover that there is something fishy going on.

I almost feel sorry for him, almost.

I hesitate for a moment before saying, You could, for example, try looking for her at the end of the students' hallway.

Pause.

In the wellness department.

He doesn't know where that is, so I'll just have to explain it to him.

He blows hot air into his hands before continuing on his way with those crooked hips of his.

He is moving faster than ususal, it seems to me, and makes creaking sounds against the loose gravel as he does so.

Good luck, I shout to him and, with his back to me, he raises his hand as a thank you gesture.

I Turn Up the Heat Even More

so that steam rises from the cabin when it ten minutes later is finally time for my shower. I have just enough time to do it before the boys call and for once the water temperature in the pipes feels right.

But I can't really enjoy it because I am begining to doubt myself. Shouldn't I have warned Birger-Bo? I regret it a little. But only just a little. I mean, he's gotta learn the truth some time, right? We can't just run away from these things. They don't just disappear because you don't like them. And what about Tom for that matter? Should he really die in ignorance and bring up another man's child? Well, that all depends on Amina. And wasn't Tom a big ape of a male back in his time? I believe he was. And why shouldn't he have been? We humans aren't so different from the animals when it comes down to it. When I peeked into the wellness area it was like watching a scene from the animal kingdom. There will always be some male animal concealing himself behind a tree in order to refine his dirty, seductive skills. That is nature's course. If you leave your female mate for so much as a single fragment of a second, just so you can go to work or collect food, the intruding male will tip toe out and grab a hold of her. He'll take care of her, making the entire forest including your dream bed, shake, because things go fast with him, there is no time for any tenderness or compassion. No, because those are the things that you, the idiot and the collector of food, wil have to attend to when you return home with your arms filled with healthy fruits.

I'm not saying that Morten was actually hiding behind a tree, but it's not far from the truth. I never did understand how it took place, but suddenly he emerged when we lived in Slagelse and our marriage happened to be in a slump. Lone was pushing on her with her law degree getting excellent grades and I was deeply buried in my master's thesis. I must admit that the topic "The Military Contribution of Danish Market Towns in the Middle Ages up until the Absolute Monarchy of 1660" perhaps wasn't the best choice. Really, how dumb can you be? I wouldn't be surprised if it had been a topic that would have appealed to Birger-Bo, but for me it meant that things went totally adrift and I didn't really feel like I was getting anywhere with it.

Was that my own fault? Would things have ended differently if I had fought more and not given Lone so much freedom? I'll never forget the day she came home and said she had decided to move into the little apartment in town her company owned. Okay, I said, if it can't be any different. She needs time, I said to myself instead of pressuring her. What if I had said that we need to stick together, you and I, if for nothing else, then for the sake of our sons? There is no way of knowing, but it's interesting to think about because suddenly Morten came into the picture and it was too late. He came riding on a white horse and an eye for her, lots of money in his saddlebag and his spiky hair and his career on the national team which wasn't quite as glamorous as he made it seem. How can you hold a candle to that? I certainly couldn't, so it was suddenly no longer about keeping the family togethr any more, but about getting a divorce and divding the property, bottled fallen fruit and the devil knows what else.

What Now?

The telephone lying next me on the sofa and which is being charged is indicating that someone is trying to get a hold of me.

It is Milovan, Yes, of course, he was going to try to get in touch at some point. I knew that, But why right now? I don't feel that I really have the energy for it, yet still I take the telephone, hold it up against my ear.

Yes? I say.

He sounds angry, there is no doubt about that. But I can't really hear what he's saying because it sounds as though he is standing in an open space of some sort. By the water, perhaps? It is wheezing and rattling. Either the connection is really bad or it's the wind. Is he out fishing? Or perhaps he is standing out on a field just outside the school.

Are you there, Milovan? I can't really hear what you're saying.

For a moment it sounds like he is speaking Serbian and that he is showeirng me with curses and damnations.

I, of course, have no doubt that the bomb has now been set off and that Amina has told him that I am aware that they have been sharing secrets so great that they would destroy everyone around them should it ever come out.

Milovan continues rambking on the other end and I recall his grayish-pale expression that emits something powerful yet at the same time oddly cold. I say in a slow and clear voice that it's no use shouting at one another from each his end of an impossible telephone conneciton but that I will be sure to send his clogs back, wherupon I click him off.

Up in My Room I Hang the Wet Towel on the Radiator.

I go over to the window and take a look outside. The courtyard is completely empty. I wonder how Birger-Bo has taken it? I sort of regret what I said, but there's no changing that now. On the other hand, what can we learn from that? That the truth is bound to reach the surface sooner or later.

Then I open the computer and light two candles on the dresser in the background so the room looks a little cozy, I don't want the boys thinking that I'm incapable of enjoying my own company.

The photograph of Knud Rasmussen which I have hung up on the wall with thumb tacks also needs to be included in the image. The portrait is absolutely incredible.

Some might say that Knud is wearing a bit too much fur and bear skins for their taste, nevertheless he has a firm gaze that emits a sense of calmness and strength. The picture tells us that we are encountering a man who is willing to hi risks.

It is only 2:51 pm, so I open one of the two bottles of rum that were forgotten on the bus, take the glass from the shelf below the bathroom mirror and pour about 3-4 centiliters, because it might help to loosen up a little after everything that's taken place. I sit down at the desk under the window and open the computer, click on the Skype app.

2:45 pm.

The rum is really fantastic and the label is very impressive-looking with a sailing ship from back when liqour was brought home from the Danish colonies in the Caribbean. You can't help wondering how many slaves could be squeezed below a single deck because Denmark, afterall, did participate in the Trans-Atlantic slave trade. Huge amounts of African slaves were bought at the Gold coast wherupon they would be sailed across the Atlantic where they would sweat and toil on the sugar cane plantations so that we could enjoy a glass of Rum like this one back home in Denmark. Naturally, it' no longer like that, something which those who have created the label and the Rum perhaps ought to bear in mind. But it tastes good, there is no denying that.

2:59 pm.

Maybe he's dangerous, considering everything he's got in his baggage, I mean. He had even done some rather serious things when he participated in the civil war in ex-Yogoslavia. From what I could surmise from the story he told me, he had been sniper, He had been lying in an abandoned office in the center of Srebrenica and shot at everything that so much as moved. According to him, he was excellent at hitting his targets from a far distance, which I know perfeclty well what means, it means that he managed to hit a lot of people, young, old, men women, children.

What do I know? Only that it is completely different from shooting animals in Poland because the massacre in Srebrenica was one of the worst we have ever seen in the history of mankind, atleast since the Nazis. It was old resentment between two peoples which had been bubbling under the surface and which finally managed to gain strength and explode and when it did it was unstoppable.

And Milovan still has a little bit of that in him, you can sense it.

Do I really have to start looking over my shoulder all the time? I doubt it, yet I can't feel 100% safe, so now is the time to be as hard as steel and not give in, even though I still feel sore in my muscles and tendons.

But then imagine Knud's pain when he walked across the ice agaisnt a stubborn, hard wind with half-dead dogs and traveling companions who just kept moaning and complaining.

But a shrill sound tells me that somebody is now calling me. Then I place the glass so it isn't visible to the camera lense.

Both Boys Look a Little Disapppointed, I Can Tell

but, on the other hand, there isn't much that can be done about it. It's the thing about Thailand. I've told them that, on second thought, I'm not so sure that it's a good idea for them to leave during my week at the Easter break.

There is a reason why we've aranged for it to be every other week, I say.

But we're skipping that now, too, Casper says. You've taken two weeks in Jultand.

Precisely, Casper, and if we were to continue in that vain who's to tell how it would all end? We could go on and on like that.

Rasmus hasn't said anything for a long time and now he looks downright sad.

I sense Lone tip-toeing and pricking up her ears in the background. I actually really don't know whether skyping with the boys is such a good idea when they are at Lone's like they are now. It feels as though I am monitoing their life. I can, for example, see that they have dragged a huge tree inside the apartment which almost reaches the ceiling and at one point I heard Lone say that they had forggotten to buy butter to which

Morten had responded rather exaggeratedly with an
"Oh, no!"

Well, go out and buy some butter, then, damnit. I
mean, is that really so hard? There must be some kiosk
or gas station that's open now and you certainly have
the legs for it, don't you? And by the way, there's no
need for you to put on airs like that to demonstrate
what a perfect life you have managed to create with
one another. As opposed to what we had together back
then. Lone and me.

You said yes, Kasper says, almost sounding
desperate.

One says a lot of things, I answer.

*

I sit looking at the empty screen when the call is
through.

It's the second time I am spending Christmas
without the boys since they were born and naturally
it's hard on everyone. It's not easy which is probably
why we get tend to get off on the wrong track with one
another.

I don't believe that Lone really loves Morten. Not for
a single second. I mean, the man wears a digital Seiku

watch that resembles something from 1984. In reality, it's just a very practical and efficient partnership they have entered into with one another in which the focus is on material goods and their careers.

At the same time, Lone contains something more, a human core, which I believe Morten is trying to take away from her. I remember she had this habit of smiling with her eyes closed. Not only when she slept but just every now and then, quite suddenly, when she was in the middle of doing something, laundry, for example. Or when she was drinking her coffee in the morning, holding the mug with both hands. It was in those moments that I loved her the most, because it was then that the engine that today just continues to run ceaselessly within her would stand still.

Merry Christmas!

Harris says as she lifts her glass of sherry. All we members of the staff do the same. The Christmas dinner will be served in a little under an hour and of course there is enough time to toast and wish everyone a Merry Christmas.

I have a hard time getting the sherry down because sherry is and will always be a sweet and sticky substance. At least compared to what I drank last night and the good little glass of Rum I just had before coming here.

The low thatch-roofed house which we are in right now is the last of the many official residences which were once affiliated with the højskole. The others have either been sold or torn down.

I talk a little with Ian, not that I feel really like it, but in fairly intelligible Danish he tells me that he used to run a lot back home in England, several marathons, in fact.

I feel a message beep in my pocket. What's this? Milovan has tried to get a hold of me a couple of more times now, however it's not Milovan I want to talk with, but Amina. But she apparently has chosen to stay in the background. It's not so good that she has contacted him. I should have seen that coming. But done is done.

How about you? Ians asks. Maybe it's something for you, too?

What?

Running.

I answer that I prefer running when the weather gets better. It's too lousy in the winter for running. He totally agrees with me. And then he wants to know whether I plan to remain at the højskole, whether I see a future for myself here, in which case there are some good, long runs you can take in the surrounding area.

Before I get a chance to respond, Harris, who is, naturally, wearing an elf hat, starts to say a few words in which she announces that she feels the urge to summarize how everything is going because, in fact, things aren't going all too well.

She shakes her head so violently that her elf hat is about to fall off.

Everyone fidgets around a little when she explains that it is the Chinese students that are the main cause of concern. The main cause, because there are, in fact, also other things. But if we address the issue with the Chinese students first, then they didn't attend church this afternoon which she is actually willing to let go because , as she says, why should they be dragged through the Christmas hymns in the hymn book, and it's also good that they aren't playing computer games so much anymore, nevertheless, her general impression is that they have "opted out."

So, looking forward we're going to have to think in new ways and in that regard she has her trepidations about the excursion planned for Wednesday because what can the Chinese students possibly get out of it?

And, by the way, where is Dennis? She adds, looking around.

It is the man from Gram who is named Dennis and I think he is the one who has planned the coming excursion which will go to the Danish Nursing History Museum.

Apparently no one knows where he is and I don't say anything.

I can still feel beeping vibrations from my phone but I can't get myself to take it out of my pocket and see what it is.

Harris turns her gaze to me. You and Dennis are the ones who have the most interaction with the Chinese students and since Dennis isn't here I'd like to ask your opinion as to what might be an intersting activity both for them and for us.

Now I'm in deep water, I'm totally blank, I must admit, but for want of anything better I suggest, surprising even myself, Knud Rasmussen's House, I mean, I have to say somethign and I realize it might come across as though I'm obsessed with Knud. I don't dare think about how long it migth take to travel to Hundested with one of the long, slow busses, whether equipped with toilets or not. The other musuem is located at Koldingborg Fjord.

Harris looks directly at me. For a moment I expect her to ask me whether my suggestion is meant as a joke, whether I can hear just how stupid it sounds, but then she suddenly brightens up into a big smile.

I Pour Plenty of Brown Sauce on My Roast Pork

because if they know how to cook anything around here in southern Jutland, aside from cake, it's brown sauce with stock and brown gravy. I pass on the the sliced carrots and cabbage heads. They taste too much of industrialized kitchen.

I return to my seat.

Birger-Bo and Elvira aren't here. In general, we aren't very many here in the dining room. There are also several who have gone home to thier families and there may be quite a number celbrating Christmas in Rynkeby which, from what I understand, is the name given to the senior homes. Those of us who have remained here tonight talk about the children, grandchildren and other family members we know we should have been together with. There are proabbly many reasons why things ended up the way they did but we chose to keep that to oursleves. We all have our own stories.

I still don't know what's happened to my mother, it is, afterall, Christmas Eve. I had hoped that it was either her or Amina who had tried to get a hold of me, but it hadn't been. It was a message from Lone who had now receievd the news from the boys that I was trying to ruin their Easter vacation. She is furious because

I had initially agreed to it and they have now bought plane tickets, made reservations, etc, etc. Let's just concentrate on celebrating Christmas and then we'll talk about it afterward, I have written, to which she hasn't responded.

I have tried to call my mother a few times. And she hasn't been active on Facebook, either. At least she hasn't made any updates since Thursday and she hasn't strewn a whole lot of likes about on the page "Frederiksværk back in the Day" as she normally does. You and I may not care the least whether the old Irma supermarket used to be located in Nord Center Mall or on Nørregade, but for those who do it is of the utmost significance. And my mother does.

Has she started drinking again? Is that what it is?

In which case all I have to say is: poor dog.

*

Aren't you going to have a slice of duck, Harris, who is sitting across from me asks. It is organic and free-range. Well, perhaps it's not quite as free-range as it used to be, Harris adds, laughung at her own joke. It's the second time she has asked me that question and I almost feel tempted to take a slice or two just to please her because the red carpet tends to get rolled out every time I make a suggestion. For example, now we are going to go to Knud Rasmussen's House, regardless of whether it turns out to be a long bus ride or not. We are going up to Hundested, and that's that.

But I don't like duck. I simply can't get it down. It all started when I was very little and my father still worked at the Danish Steelworks Company. One day he came home and said: Guess what? Today we're going to have a duck from the countryside, that is, a duck that has consumed grain and dirtied itself on a dung hill. And we were immediately on board because it sounded much more enticing than those dull cardboard ducks mom always brought home from the refrigerated counter in the supermarket.

A few days before Christmas Eve the farmer called and asked whether we'd also be interested in seeing the duck get slaughtered. I think we'll skip that, my father had said. When the roast came out of the oven Christams Eve it was brown and crispy and looked delicious but as soon as we sank our teeth into it there was a peculiar aftertaste. Of mud. Or of something earthy.

We immediatey realized what the problem was: it tasted too much of duck, which was something we weren't used to. And I still feel that way now. Life has become too raw and brutal for my taste. I wouldn't mind if it was more insipid and monotonous and tasted a little more of cardboard duck.

I Hear the Sound of a Car Door Slam Shut

when I go out to the courtyard after dinner and the others are dancing around the Christmas tree in the gym. I stop in my tracks. Who could it be who's taking off now? I mean, it is, afterall, Christmas Eve. The sound came from the parking lot behind the main building. I start walking in that direction.

It's turned cold, which I like, and there are only a few clouds in the sky. It may not be a white Christmas this year but when does that ever really happen? When I turn the corner of the building I catch sight of a Berlingo in the row of cars, the lights of which are turned on and the trunk is open.

A small yellow light is also switched on in the passenger compartment, I notice, and someone is sitting in there. In the passenger seat. I stick close to the wall of the building as I slowly nch closer. It is Elvira. She is weeping with her loose, wrinkly mouth and an expression of utter despair on her vulnerable face.

What's going on?

The trunk is open. The car radio must be on because I can hear the song "Last Christmas" with Wham playing softly in the background.

Shut it off, damn it! It's unbearable to listen to!

Where is Birger Bo? Seeing her like this is upsetting.

I am just about to go all the way to the car when the door by the staircase to the main house opens and Birger Bo comes out carrying a piece of luggage in each hand.

What's going to happen now? They are leaving. That's what they are going to do. He doesn't want to be here anymore. It was too much for him to handle.

Birger Bo tosses the luggage in the back of the car and sits down in the driver's seat. He doesn't so much as look at Elvira which makes her weep even more. I can't hear it and, fortunately, I can't hear Wham any longer either because he starts the car and backs up, Birger-Bo, as he rests one of his arms on the back of Elvira's seat. I just manage to see her cover her face with her hands before the yellow light goes out.

At least he takes her along home with him, I think, as I watch the car disappear. That's a good sign. He isn't just going to let it pass, like I did. But that was before I came across Knud.

The car sure is ugly. It looks more or less like the back of a cow.

Imagine,
It Is Actually Possible
to Drown Crabs

Exactly What Do You think You Are Doing?

Amina asks in a trembling voice.

Nothing, I answer as calmly and with as much confidence as possible.

But I'm certainly happy that you finally decide to call, I add.

The sliding doors with the ads for multi-grain bread on sale posted on them open as I approach them. I am walking out of the Superbrugsen in Rødding and am on my way back to the højskole. The staff meeting will start in ten minutes in Harris' office. I have bought a pair of underwear because when I went over to the school's laundromat this morning I couldn't tell which compartment was for the soap and which was for the fabric softener in the washing machine and I didn't feel like asking anyone.

Hello? Are you there?

Yes, I'm still here allrigt, I answer as I rummage through some items on discount displayed outside the store: door mats, bird food, wood briquettes. It's the first day Since Christmas that the shops are open again so there are a lot of people out shopping.

I am perfectly aware of the fact that I have the upper hand here so I keep Amina hanging on the line a little. She hasn't so much as even mentioned the picture yet.

I hear her mention something about me taking advantage of her trust after she had actually shared one of her most private secrets with me and thereby opened her heart to me.

I feel like saying that it apparently hadn't just been her heart she had opened through the years but I decide against it. She says she can't get over just how sick my actions are and that she certainly had never suspected me of being a stalker until now.

A stalker? Well, that's definitely not the case, I am just about to say in my defense, but then I remember that she, of coure, does have one thing that she can use against me and that is that I was tip-toeing around her yard while the next door neighbor was watching me.

I tell her that depsite the fact that those things may be true she must believe me when I say that the only thing I'm interested in right now is that that backpack is returned to its rightful owner and as soon as that's done we can all go back to our lives and forget any of this ever happened.

Neither of us has mentioned the picture with so much as a single word and before she gets a chance to answer I announce that the højskole will actually be coming to Hundested the day after tomorrow, to which she responds with silence.

The day after tomorrow? she then says.

Yes, so I was thinking I would drop by and pick up the backpack and then you won't have to give it another thought.

Well, it'll have to be before five, then.

Why?

Because Tom is at his family's place with the kids and he'll be coming home around that time.

Okay, that's fine. No problem.

Now All We Need Is to Take Care of the Documentaiotn for Traveling Expenses,

Harris announces as one of the first items on the agenda at the start of the meeting. She slowly looks around the staff table. The fact is, she explains, that when she checked the Mayland calendar this moring, which has its regualr place in the top drawer of the writing desk, the mileage didn't match up with the information on the dahsboard.

Now why does she have to bring that up? Wasn't it tomorrow's trip that we were going to quickly run through? I have been in contact with Knud Rasmussen's House, the big bus equipped with toilets and the whole thing is scheduled to arrive at 9 am sharp. So everything is ready and set to go. But of course somone like Harris would notice the slighest idiosyncracy because that's the way she is. Even though everybody knows that Harris herself has been known to take the car every now and then when she had to make a quick errand to the nursery together with her Brit.

I pretend to be deeply engrossed in my phone, which I in all honesty actually am because my mother's neighbor has called my sister and told her that she has checked in on our mother, as promised. What doesn't one do for one's fellow humans? It's the same woman who prohibited my mother from entering the retirement club and who reported her to the management because she had been running around naked on the common grounds.

So I don't entirely trust her words. At any rate, she told my sister that there was no answer when she rang the doorbell and that the persian blinds were rolled down.

All of this took place over an hour ago, so something's got to be done soon. But what can I do? Should I call the police? Is that what this has come down to now? I guess if I don't do it that busybody of a neighbor will do it herslef and that's when the troubles begin. Or at least she'll call the Animal Control, the Animal Protection Agency or whatever it's called.

My sister still has her shift at the barracks which she'll continue to have until New Year's Day.

As I place my grooved plastic cup under the tall thermo pot standing in the middle of the table I discover that the language teacher is giving me a look indicating that he knows perfectly well that I am the one who has taken the car for those extra kilometers.

Has he compltely lost his mind? My mistake is ridiculously tiny compared to what he did. Does he really have no shame? No, probably not. But I do and it is haunting me. I'll never forget the sight of Elvira and Birger Bo driving off in their round Berlingo that resembles a cow.

I take a sip of lukewarm coffee and try to forget him but he continues to stare at me.

Does anyone happen to know where Elvira and Birger Bo are? I ask while returning the language teacher's gaze.

When the Meeting Is Over and Everyone's Left

I sneak into the mail and copying room behind the office. There must be enough time for that. I manage to find some leftover wrapping paper from Christmas Eve. I also find an empty box in which there used to be copying paper. I place the brand-new clogs in it. I bought them earlier today in the supermarket. But the box is, of course, much too big. They'll just rattle around in there. I should have known that. But there's nothing to do about it because there are no other boxes that I can find.

Let's see. I start filling up the space in the box with old newspapers that I find lying in a pile on one of the shelves. I hope they aren't newspapers that have been saved because they contain important articles. I really doubt that. It's just Harris who can't really get herself to throw anything away. Even a dirty, empty aquarium filled with algae on the inside hasn't been taken to the recycling center, I notice. It has been left on the top shelves together with old ink cartridges. I know it once stood in the palm garden but it was too much of a hassle to have to remember to feed the fish and clean it.

I also once had an aquarium. I got it for my birthday when I turned twelve. I will never forget something that took place in the aquarium once. I had been out fishing in Lynæs with my father and because we did't manage to catch anything we placed some crabs in a pail of water because we had to come home with something. They were then placed in the aquarium. The crabs. They started running sideways on the stone bottom, causing confusion among the fish but the next morning the roles had been switched. All the crabs were dead and the fish swam up close to them and nibbled on their legs, eyes and antennae, wherever they could get to them, as though they knew that the crabs no longer posed a threat. I didn't understand a thing. Not until later did I realize that the crabs must have drowned because they hand't been able to crawl up the slippery sides to get air They can't survive in water like that for an endless amount of time. But imagine, you can actually drown crabs.

After I have stuffed plenty of crumpled balls of newspaper around the clogs I close the box, wrap it in wrapping paper, tape it with adhesive tape and finisih off by putting a white sticker on it upon which I have written the address and everything.

The camper. I figured out on my own where Milovan was when I woke up. He was, of course, sleeping in his beloved camper parked in the driveway. Men who live alone get the strangest ideas.

I place the box in the receptionist's office where outgoing mail is put. Our recpetionist will probably ensure that it gets sent out already today.

There. That was that. I know this had nothing to do with the clogs but I had said to him that I would send them and I don't really see why I shouldn 't. You should always keep your word, I have always lived by that motto.

I'm Wallking Around in my Room Packing My Things,

I must remember everything, I can't risk leaving a single thing behind. I know that tomorrow will be a defining day on all fronts. If everything goes as I think and hope it will, all the necessay pieces will fall into place at some point tomorrow evening. I don't see how they couldn't. I'm sure there's someone out there who might be in doubt, but let's see.

Aside from that, I have contacted that crazy woman in my mother's rental housing association and written to her that I will see to everything as soon as possible. I've told my sister the same thing. One day more or less, give or take, can't make that big a difference. After all, the dog is sure to manage. The worst thing that can happen is that it might urinate on the floor.

My phone is beeping. It's a message from Ian Harris. He wants to know if I'd like to join him in going to the swimmin pool and swimming a few laps with him since I find the weather too cold for jogging. At any rate, he is on his way down there for a swim and if I care to join him then we'll just see each other there.

I think he feels pretty lonely.

There. I think I've packed everything down now.

I close the suitcase. I don't know whether I should get the vacuum cleaner out of the closet and give the room a quick run through? No, I'll leave it alone. Once I leave this place tomorrow and start heading toward Frederiksværk and Hundested, there'll be no way back.

NEWSPAPER

It's Probably Not Nearly as Worn

as you had imagined, says the attendant, referring to Knud's kayak which is hanging from the ceiling just as it did when I was here with the boys.

I hadn't really imagined anything in particular and I actually wouldn't mind if he'd start to wrap things up right about now, the attendant, because it will soon be 4 pm and I'm starting to feel antsy.

That's because Knud's father only allowed him to paddle around a little in the fjord, the attendant continues, because should even the slightest leak arise when a hunter is far away from home and freezing cold polar water starts seeping in, you are as good as finished.

From there he starts talking about the eskimoes' hunting habits, how they primarily caught seals and fish from their kayaks but that they were most certainly also able to get nutrition in other ways.

Is he actually going to continue? He seems to be utterly unstoppable.

I look for Harris in hopes that she can assist in speeding the process up a little so we can finally get going. It turns out that she is in the room next door in which she is walking around alone. Right now she is studying a tupilaq in the windowsill, small soapstone figures that represent some very unpleasant and shapeless beings.

Aren't they delicate? she asks.

Delicate might be overdoing it, I say and suggest that it might be about time that we leave.

She nods but gives no indication that she is listening to me. She just moves the soapstone figures around a little with a big smile on her face.

She doesn't seem to have a care in the world and in a way I can understand her because both the Chinese students and the pensioners seem very enthusiastic about today's trip. And that is pretty impressive, I guess. Because, let's be honest, it's seldom that we go on an excusion for which our hearts are beating with the utmost passion. Who doesn't remember their schooldays? Today we are going to go to Æbelholt Abbey and on the way home we are scheduled ot visit a butcher in Frederikssund.

Well, at least she's forgotten all about the mileage account. Nevertheless, it seems like she won't be of much assistance in helping things move faster, so I return to the big room with the kayak.

The assistant is busy telling about how the hunters who had managed to catch a seal would immediately open the belly with a sharp knife, cull out the liver, cut it into small cubes and distribute it among them. He pretends to be eating raw and steamy seal liver with his bare hands. To be honest, it looks a little exaggerated, and somehow I almost feel like telling him that I have already informed them of all these things. Instead i make do with adding that it has to do with the fact that that was the only way they could get any C-vitamin, which , as we all know, is stored in the innards.

And now that I have taken the floor I take the opportunity to say that we really should get going now becausewe have quite a long way home, right?

The attendant says that he would just like to add that the reindeer would come out of the forest during the autumn, fat and lazy, with their newly born calves and full of meat were driven through a narrow passage which, once they were in it, they couldn't leave again.

A settlement could ensure enough stock for the winter on a single afternoon like that.

Okay, that really does sound exciting, I say as I start shooing the enthusiastic crowd toward the exit.

Goodbye, and thanks for a great tour, I say before closing the door behind me.

The old people slowly make their way to the bus that is standing and waiting with its engine running.

Harris is standing by the door and counting them as they disappear into the bus.

So far so good. I take a breath of fresh air coming in from Kattegat. I remember it from when I stood waiting for Amina at the ferry dock. You don't grow tired of it that easily.

But something's going on now. They are speaking to each other in loud voices down by the bus, Harris, and the bus driver and Ian. They are looking around and pointing as though they are searching for somethng.

Harris crawls up into the bus. Twenty seconds later she comes back out.

She starts walking in my direciton, walking as rapidly as her body will allow her on the uneven terrain.

Have you seen Malte anywhere ? she asks as she approaches me, breathless.

I shake my head.

Isn't he there?

No.

Harris looks concerned.

Damn. That's just what we need. There simply isn't time for this.

I'm sure he's here somewhere, I say, trying to conceal my iritatiton.

We get the last particpants into the bus, disperse and start searching. Harris and Ian run around on the grounds among the wind-swept trees and bushes. The bus driver, who is rather stout, runs down toward a wooden staircase by the hard cliff leading down to the beach.

No, let's just hope that Malte didn't go down there thinking we all should go out bathing. The ocean, which is as calm as a gray steel surface, must be freezing cold.

I myself run back to the house, knock on the door but there is no response.

Then I catch sight of Knud Rasmussen's work house located a little ways inland. The lights are on and the door is ajar.

Actually, the house is supposed to be locked up due to renovation. Teh attandeant said it was supposed to get painted and wallpapered but apparenly somebody's down there.

I rush down to the house.

I push open the door and immediately catch sight of him.

He is sitting stark naked, pale and wrinkled and with liver spots on one of the polar bear hides Knud must have transported home from Greenland, yes, the room is stuffed with things, photographs, topogical maps, dried plants and many more things from his expeditions.

Malte, damnit!

Naturally, I Sit Down Next to the Bus Driver

who has a small tag which says Bruno on it.

We nod to each other, Bruno and I. He puts the car into gear, releases the clutch and we are on our way. And it's actually not a second too early because it is now ten to five.

We don't drive very far before we pass a sign indicating that we are leaving Hundested and entering Sølager.

It's time now. I lean over to Bruno and whisper something no one else can hear. He nods while keeping his eyes on the road. As a bus driver he's probably used to clients suddenly getting strange ideas from time to time, so Bruno just does what he's asked to do without giving it much thought. He turns on the left-hand signal, pulls over and stops at the foot of Rønnebærvej. I take the microphone, which is located right below the front windowshield. I click on the little button so it lights up green.

I'll be back in a second, I say. I just have to get something, and then I'll be back.

Bruno releases the punp that gets the front door of the bus to open and I jump down on the cement before anyone has a chance to stop me. Without looking back I start to slowly walk up the hill. There are tall fences and when I reach Amina's house there are no cars parked in the driveway. Tom has apparnetly not come home yet and everything is going as planned.

I Didn't Want To Do It

Amina says, her voice sounding almost a little shrill.

No, but it doesn't matter now, I say.

It's Tom, okay? That's the way he gets when he gets carried away.

We're standing in the kitchen, Amina and me, the air is full of tension because I have no idea what's going on in her mind, I can't read her at all. She is wearing a thin white shirt and I'm not sure whether she is wearing a bra underneath. What's that supposed to mean?

She has also just gotten her hair cut, I notice, except that her hair seems dry. I think she may have perhaps dyed her hair.

You have to believe me when I say that I've always felt there was something special between you and me that goes back to those days ...

She disrupts herself, covers her face with her hands and shakes her head.

I check the time. It's 5:07 pm. Tom could be here any moment. As a matter of fact, he should have been here by now.

Suddenly I change moods entirely, what the hell has gotten into her?

Shut up, damnit! I shout, making her start.

I am just as taken aback by my outburst as she is, but

this is now my new self speaking and I'm getting really tired of listening to her.

And once I lose my temper I can't control it and I so I tell her that I know perfectly well that the only reason she chose Tom, that big stupid oaf, was because he worshipped her and in her naivity she thought that he could defend her against the Milovans of the world but it's no use because neither Tom nor anyone else can defend her against what's already inside of her. And I'm just grateful it wasn't me who was the unfortunate man to hit jackpot and condemned to spend the rest of my life with the likes of her.

But if you would be so kind as to go get the thing that you know perfeclty well that I've come for I would be very grateful, I say in a very different and milder tone of voice.

We might as well get it over with, right?

Amina slowly nods and disappears down the hallway.

About a half minute passes. Maybe a little more.

I think I hear a car. I run over to the hallway and look through the windowpane on the front door. Is that Tom pulling up into the driveway? No, it was just a random car.

Why isn't she coming? And where's the dog. Anyway? He probably took it with him to Ringsted.

I look down the dark, empty hallway and then I shout: Amina!

There is no response.

Are you coming or what?

I'm just about to shout again when I see Amina coming out of the door down there holding the backpack in her arms.

I catch myself smiling.

She is walking rapidly and determinedly toward me as though she has spent some time collecting herself. She has also covered her shouldes with a cardigan.

She stops a few meters away from me and carefully places the backpack on the floor.

I can sense thats he would like to say something but she can't seem to get the words out. Her cheeks are wet.

Suddenly she looks in the living room and her facial expression changes. I don't know what she's seen.

What is it? I ask as I rush over to where she's standing. I look into the living room and further out to the yard where I see Tom making his way toward the panorama window. So it *was* him that I heard afterall a little while back ago. He must have parked out on the street and tip-toed round the house. This was precisely what wasn't supposed to happen. Is she more cunning than I thought? Have they devised all of this beforehand?

My eyes automatically start looking for something that I can use as a weapon.

In the kitchen they have a row of knives hanging from a magnet on a metal rail above the kitchen bench. We immediately make eye contact, Tom and I. The expression in his eyes are so full of rage that my stomach turns to ice, but only momentarily, because I now take action by grabbing the backpack, charging toward the front door, tearing it open, continuing out to the driveway, grab a hold of one of the carpport posts and practically swing myself out onto the residential road.

I run as fast as I possibly can, which isn't much, I should have gone out jogging with Ian afterall.

The bus is waiting at the bottom of the hill.

I glance over my shoulder.

Tom is now also out on the street. I don't remember him being so big. He has presumably also gotten bigger with the years but that doesn't seem to have slown him down. He is moving at breathtaking speed.

I reach the bus and run along it. Through the big square windows I can see the many faces. Some of the old people lift their hands and wave enthusiastically as though they understand that something really exciting is taking place. The Chinese students, on the other hand, pretend like they don't see me. They seem to be looking straight throught me.

I Lean Forward and Rest My Hands on My Knees

and am perspiring so much that the sweat is dripping off my nose. I am still gasping for air but my pulse is on its way down.

So, I managed to escape him afterall.

He was on my heels in the old residential neighborhood by the big realtor, he was very close at that point, but then I found a detour where newer buildings have been built among the older ones and doscovered a dirt road leading to a creek. I jumped across it and ran up toward Ullerup Forest where I am now. Up on a hillcrest without trees.

It's pretty amazing!

I sit down on a bench with the backpack on my lap and enjoy the view for a moment. I can see Isjafjord and the cape. And a riding school. A rider is pulling his horse toward a training ground upon which obstacles have been set up.

I'm going to have to give Harris a call, she was stadndign at the bus door when I ran past them and she shouted something to me. I take out my phone.

Hello? Hi, Betram, what's going on? She asks before I get a chance to say anything.

I tell her that that which they witnesed was no big deal, just a mere private dispute which has now been cleared up.

She says that she is happy to hear that. She also says that they are still waiting for me in the bus and that they'd like to start heading toward Jutland now.

My mother needs me, I hear myself say. I fear that she might be dead in her house because her drinking problem has started to take over her life again.

It's been awhile since anyone's been in contact with her, I say.

Harris asks whether I plan to return to Rødding, I can tell by the tone of her voice that she already knows the answer to that question.

Say hi to Ian and say that I'm sure Dennis would be more than willing to go swimming with him.

We hang up.

I sit for a moment and collect myself. Ha ha. Serves them well. That'll teach 'em.

I suddenly notice some strange, snapping sounds so I look down toward the riding school because that's where they seem to be coming from. At first I think they're from when the horses topple over the partitions on the obstacle course, but they're not. It's Tom. He's going from one stable door to the next along a long wing with thatched roofs and I know what he's up to. He is checking the stalls to see if I am hiding in one of them.

Damn, Damn, Damn!

I was certain I had managed to shake him off, but now he's making his way up the hill in my direction, stooping heavily, like a bear close to defeat, so I grab my backpack and rush off.

My feet move with tremendous speed, down, down, down the slope.

But I'm going a little too fast and just before I reach the bottom I manage to slip on some squashy leaves, I fall, get back on my feet, and continue running.

Shit! The backpack! I dropped it. I have to go back. There! Got it!

I conitnue running, on and on.

I run among the trees that don't provide much protection this time of year, I can sense that he is right behind me.

Suddenly the forest floor becomes soup-like and swampy, a low terriain of melting water. I start to sink down.

When I work my way through it I find a forest path which I follow, but this isn't very good. My shoes and trouser legs have gotten soaking wet and heavy and I can hear him shouting behind me.

Yeah, fuck you, Tom. But I know perfectly well. I don't stand a chance. I won't manage to escape him.

After the path has broken off, I make a quick decision, stop at the great beech tree and position myself behind the tree trunk. I know I'm really taking a huge chance here, but what else can I do? I pick up what looks to be a sturdy branch. It feels alright in my hand. I get ready. He's almost here, I can hear him.

He's breathing very heavily, blowing air out through his nose, he really does sound like an animal. He stops in his tracks, has no clue where I've gone.

As he passes the tree I'm standing next to, I slowly shuffle my feet in a backward motion around the tree trunk so that I am behind him. He towers in front of me. He is gigantic as he stands gazing across the area.

I lift the branch and at the very same moment that Tom turns I swing it, hitting him hard with a precise blow to the side of his head, putting all my body weight into it.

Thump!

He stands still for a moment, swaying back and forth, emitting a strange sound before collapsing frontward without shielding himself with his hands, his head landing directly on the forest floor.

I don't wait to see what happens with him then, oh no, I'm not sticking around for that because there's nothing more dangerous than an injured animal.

I Walk Down the Aisle of the Open Train Carriage

and find a vacant seat on one of the tall green seats. The conductor blows the whistle for departure.

My heart is still pounding at ninety miles an hour. Damn! What's gonna happen to Tom? I just left him lying there in the middle of the forest. Perhaps I shouldn't have done that. I get out my phone and write a message to Amina telling her where she can find him.

I don't think we should assume that anything serious has happened to him but I still feel an obligation to let her know. I can't believe that I actually managed to do it because this time it was genuine, the real deal, and not just a game or virtual or on some stupid playing field, but it's also got to stop here. I'm no superman and I'd prefer to be Allan-Benjamin again, even though he's now sitting here with wet shoes, socks and pants and leaving a small pile of slush on the linoleum floor.

I look around. There aren't that many passengers, but that's perhaps not so strange since it is still Christmas for most people. I still have my phone in my hand, so I send a text message to Lone. I write that I have thought about it and I have reached the conclusion that the boys shouldn't be deprived of that trip to Thailand afterall. I feel it is the right thing to do. I'm not saying that it was an easy decision to make, but it was the right one.

I rest my forehead on the filthy, dirty and cold windowpane and close my eyes for a moment.

It's going to be so wonderful once all of this is over and done with. And we're almost there. Once all of this is through, which won't be long, I'm going to see whether I can find some other more constructive way of using my capabilities. The possibilties are endless. I could open up a coffee bar. A coffee bar? Yeah, why not? I could also apply for a job at a kindergarten. It doesn't have to be anything fancy. I'm pretty good with kids. Okay, I realize I was 29 before we got Casper, but, still, I feel like I've always been around kids.

At any rate, it won't be necessary to meet up again with the case worker at the unemployment agency, he can shove it. I don't feel like seeing him sitting there looking so self-important, as though he most graciously is having to resort to bending the rules for my sake.

I open my eyes, My telephone is buzzing in my pocket. Lone has already responded. I'm happy to hear that, she writes. And she asks whether we should get together for lunch soon after I get back so we can discuss the boys a little.

I don't see why not, I answer and genuinely mean it.

When the Train Stops at Frederiksværk

I am already standing by the train door and am one of the first to step onto the platform. At the station kiosk I turn off at Strandvejen instead of continuing up toward town. There is quite a distance to walk and it is freezing cold but our mission is almost accomplished. Nevertheless, I am impatient. It was the same for Knud when he was about to reach the end of one of his expeditions, it was always the final kilometers that were the longest.

I walk past Nærkøb where when I was in 1st or 2nd grade would buy the latest Donald Duck and Co., for me and The Inquirer for you, Mom, on Wednesdays which was the day I always got off early from school. I would drink either KB hvidtøl or Jolly Cola while you would drink black coffee with sweeteners and smoke cigarettes. And if anyone had looked through one of those windows to the kitchen they would have witnessed a mother-and-son scene of joy rarely witnessed in this world. But that's so long ago. Now I am finally back where it all began because I am starting to discern see the red brick apartment complexes, their good, solid cratfstmanship. And I can now also see my mother's drawn, semi-dirty Persian blinds and heavy curtains. I want to pick up the pace but can feel myself slowing down. I have absolutely no fucking clue what I'm going to find in there.

The Door Is Indeed Locked,

however, I knock on the door a few times anyway for the sake of appearnces because there is a man in the parking lot removing snow from a front window shield with both his hands and his arms. He looks like he could be a superintendent in his blue Kansas overalls.

I patiently wait until he is through and has driven off. In order to get to the opposite side of the house I have to walk all the way around the tile path, past all the front doors decorated with Christmas wreaths, to the place where the row of low ground-floor apartments ends.

On the backside I walk back along the building until I reach my mother's apartment that seems completly closed up also on this side. In the small courtyard of two times three meters there is a blue wicker chair with steel legs and a round garden table. On the table there is a kerosene lamp and a large ashtray which I knnw Mom brought with her from the fishing house after my father died.

I walk straight ahead toward the panorama window pane, cup my eyes with my hands and try to look through the window. It's not entirely dark, a gray light is seeping in through the elongated window above the dining table from the opposite end of the house.

Perhaps an exhaust hood or something else is switched on in the kitchen. It seems like it because a little light is seeping in from the kitchen.

I think I sense some movement of some kind, something is rustling around in there. The garden gate, which is worn down and its paint peeling off, is, of course, also locked.

I don't feel there is any need for hesitation. I take one step back and hammer so hard right by the lock of the door that it burtsts open with a bang. The door frame doesn't get particularly torn. It's all made of old crap.

The stench is overwhelming, both sweet smelling and sour at the same time, like rotting fur, and there is something alive in there.

Sita, the little carpet-urinater, comes runnning toward me out from the darkness. It is so happy that someone has come that it is wagging with its entire backside.

Hey there, little one, how's it going? where's mom? I ask.

It licks my hand, its snout is gooey, as though it's found something to eat. Wherupon it continues, running out into the fresh air and I don't stop it. I find the light switch inside to the left, turn it on and take a step into the living room. I look around. There is a pair of newly purchased torqouise and orange running shoes.

Mom! I shout. Hello!

A used coffee cup is standing on the sofa table. And an overturned wine jar is lying on the floor But I don't see any glasses. Did she drink it straight from jar?

Then I catch sight of her. She is lying on the carpet by the wall next to the bureau. One of her legs is protruding from her body in a very unnatural position. Is she dead?

I rush over to her and turn her around.

Mom! Mom, damn it! Are you okay?

She seems to be completely gone. She is lying in her own vomit and gotten some of it in her hair. That's what is giving off the sour smell. It's yellow and orange and I now I realize what the dog had on his snout. It was the only thing it could consume. Maybe it tried to awaken her by licking her on her face.

I place my ear to her face. Yes, she is still breathing. But not enough, I think. Her chest is moving up and down, but just faintly.

What do I do?

Then I open one of her eyes with my thumb and index finger. Her pupils don't react. Her face is chalk-white and her lips are thin and blue. How long could she have been lying here like this?

I bend her head a good ways back and lift her chin, then I squeeze her nostrils and place my mouth against my mother's and start giving her mouth-to-mouth resuscitation.

It's really disgusting. I mean, this is my mother for Christ's sake!

Suddenly she opens up her eyes and looks at me with loathing, as though to say, "What in hell do you think you're doing?"

I pull away from her.

She keeps my eyes locked in her gaze.

Did you bring the money? She asks in her unused and horse sounding voice. I can see that she must have fallen. She has a bruise on her temple.

Yes, mother, I brought the money, I answer, placing the backpack on the floor next to her.

Here you go!

Then I get up and go out to the bathroom. I let the door stay open. I turn on the faucet, check the temperature of the water with my hand and find some towels.

Yes, Mother, we're gonna get you back on your feet in no time. First you're going to have a nice warm bath and then we'll give the apartment a good and thorough cleaning.

I love you, Mother, like only a son can love you. After all, I once came out of you. Yes, Mom is the best in the world. She has taken care of you in every possible way. Wiped your behind and your mouth, rocked you to sleep, and it will stick with you to doom's day, to the day you die, and the temperature is now just about right.

I look at her through the open bathroom door. She is sitting up and is unzipping the backback. She sticks her hand down into it. When it comes back up it is not holding the stack of bills that I picked up from Handels Bank a while back ago.

She looks goofishly at me with one of her eyes shut. She shakes the piecesof newspaper which she is holding in her hand up in the air as though to say, "What the hell is this?" Her mouth is salivating.

I can easily tell you, Mom, because it can only be pieces of newspaper money that Tom and Amina must have carefully cut out from the Frederiksborg local newspaper so they could really do a number on me, as though no one has ever done a number on anyone before, and if it wasn't for the fact that the whole thing is so damn tragic it would actually have been funny, like when Knud survives the wildest expeditions and shoots polar bears and wolves just so he can come back home, lie down and die of a common lung infection, 'cause you can never win, you just can't. All you can do is accept the fact that the universe is laughing at you, making it echo in all the terazzo staircases in all the neighborhoods of the world.

Nina Sokol is a poet and translator in the midst of translating novels, short stories. plays and poems by Danish writers. She was a grant poet-in-residence at The Vermont Studio Center in 2011. She has received several grants from the Danish Art's Council to translate plays, including a play written by the fairy tale writer H.C. Andersen which was published by the journal "InTranslation." Her own poems have appeared in American journals, including Miller's Pond and the Hiram Poetry Review and a collection is now available from Spuyten Duyvil, The *Silence Sound Makes*.